Missing Dad

Missing Dad

6. Ransom

J. Ryan

CHAPTER 1

The Black Knight

Time seems to have stood still since I was last in this small country churchyard with Tommaso. Paying our respects at the simple granite stone that marks the final resting place of his father. With gentle breezes blowing and a calm, clouded sky, it's so quiet here. Becks and I step back to leave Tommaso with his thoughts as he gazes at the grey stone. After a few moments, he turns to us with a slight smile. 'This is a good place. I think he is at peace at last.'

We're back in the hired Ford, heading down the M5, when the idea comes to me. 'Look, there's hours before we have to be at the airport. Why don't we take in the Bristol suspension bridge?' I've told Tommaso about how some of the best and the worst times of my life were spent on that old bridge.

His face lights up. 'I would like that very much!'

There are no gentle breezes blowing here, three hundred feet above the River Avon. The gusts whip Becks' mane of red hair and make my eyes water. Tommaso looks intently down as the brown, swirling water licks the muddy banks. 'So this is where you first saw Monsieur?'

'I must have been very small. Couldn't see over the top of the bridge! I was holding Dad's hand and he was waving at this yachtsman …'

'In the Lisette.' Becks brushes her hair out of her eyes. 'That must have been when your dad and Monsieur were working together.'

'There's so much of Dad's past that I know absolutely nothing about.' Little did I know then how much of that was about to change.

Monsieur meets us in the arrivals area of Marseille Marignane airport. I notice that there's a slight tenseness about him, in the way that he's scanning the crowds around us. He walks us briskly to the Bentley and the door locks snap shut as soon as we're all seated. 'Did it go well?'

Tommaso replies, 'Very well, thank you, Monsieur. And is all well at L'Étoile?' So he's noticed, too.

'At L'Étoile, yes. But there has been a development which Julius and I will tell you about.'

Knowing Monsieur's mastery of the art of understatement, we all exchange looks and my stomach tightens.

Monsieur insists on everyone eating before he and Dad put us in the picture. And despite the sense of looming trouble, we all attack the food ravenously as it's been ages since our last meal. I ask Mum, 'Where's Jack?'

'He had his tea early – huge pile of homework. Arnaud and Talia are away on a course.' Her face has a tenseness that I've not seen in a long time; that old fear about Dad has come back. Soon after, she leaves the dining room, her plate barely touched. With a sudden loss of appetite, I put down my knife and fork.

After the meal, we all go into Monsieur's study. Dad is looking far from his usual devil-may-care self. Tommaso looks as though he knows what Dad is going to say; I guess, with his background in the Camorra, he knows more than most of us.

Monsieur begins, 'First, I must inform you that all the security systems here are going to be continuously activated for the foreseeable future. We will also be regularly deploying the Velociraptor in the skies around the château. In addition, we have a radar system located within the roof which can be operated remotely from here in my office.'

Dad flicks on the screen of Monsieur's desktop computer and there's the green display, scanning the skies above us. He continues the narrative. 'We're telling you this first, guys, because we could come under attack at any time. What we're going to tell you now is from whom, and why.' He takes the ruby memory stick from his pocket and plugs it into the desktop. Taps the keyboard and brings up an image.

The man whose face we're looking at is maybe mid-thirties. A pleasant enough expression; quite studious, with thick-rimmed glasses. Slightly balding. 'Do you all remember, when you were searching through this memory stick for clues, my reference to the Black Knight?'

Becks says, 'Yes – thanks to you he was serving time at Her Majesty's pleasure, wasn't he?'

Dad's blue eyes are serious. 'Was, yes.'

'You mean, he's escaped?'

'I'm afraid so, Becks.'

'When was this, Dad?'

'Last night, Joe.'

'How did he get out?'

'A small army of mercenaries arrived by helicopter, stormed the prison and blasted their way back out, taking him with them.'

'Were people hurt?'

'Fortunately, not seriously. But there was the potential for serious harm.'

'You worked undercover for this Black Knight before you got the job with the Contessa, didn't you Dad?'

'Correct, Joe.'

'Was it the same kind of work, like, bodyguard?'

'Broadly the same …'

'And he was a drugs baron?'

'On the face of it, he was the highly respectable chief executive of a pharmaceutical company.'

'Like, the ones who've got tens of thousands of Americans hooked on opioids?'

'Perfectly legally, yes: although many like you and I consider it homicidally criminal. But opioids weren't the only drugs being brewed up in his labs.'

'Cocaine?'

'Heroin. The most frequent cause of death among consumers of illegal drugs in his home city of Berlin.'

Becks frowns. 'I'd never thought of Europe as a major drug-trafficking area.'

'That's because most of the publicity focuses on the US, Becks. Germany – in particular Berlin and Dortmund – is the drugs capital of Europe. Organised crime has a stranglehold.'

'And this guy was running it all?'

'Most of it. And making billions, Becks. His heroin commanded a high price, and he had a well-organised distribution network.'

'What's his real name, Dad?'

Dad brings up another image. This time, the Black Knight is socialising at what looks like a high society event, champagne flute in hand. 'Dieter von Schwarzberg is an extremely charming sort. To look at him, you'd never think that behind those benevolent features is a mind focused totally on control. And prepared to do anything to keep it.'

'Like, killing people?'

'He prefers to keep his own hands clean. But he has plenty of well-paid hitmen.'

'How long did you work for him, before you landed him in jail?'

'It took two years to gather all the evidence we needed. He was a very slippery character. Highly intelligent.'

'Was it difficult to get the job?' I'm thinking back to Dad's account on the ruby memory stick of how he had to deal with the Contessa's hitman.

'Not at all. You see, Joe, we were at university together. I'd known Dieter for quite a while.'

'You were friends?'

'Acquaintances. Enough for him to feel that I could be useful to him.'

'But didn't he know about you in the SAS …?'

Dad smiles ironically. 'And, as with the Contessa, that meant I came highly recommended. They love special forces who've turned …'

'Except that you hadn't …'

'That's the great game of going undercover, Joe. Your new boss has to see you as his own. He has to believe that you would sacrifice your life to save his.'

'When all you want is to put him behind bars.'

'He trusted me implicitly right up until the handcuffs closed around his wrists.'

'And now he's escaped – will he just go to ground?'

'I'm afraid that's not Dieter's style, Becks. First, he'll want to settle old scores. And then he'll set up shop all over again.'

'Old scores …?'

'Yep – yours truly. And very possibly everyone close to me. That's why I need to get to him first.'

I find that I've stood up. 'No Dad. That's why you need to stay right here.'

He shakes his head. 'I thought you'd say that – but, no, Joe.'

'Have you seen what this is doing to Mum? You can't put her through all that again!'

'Neither can I sit here and let this brute terrorise my family!'

'Then I'm coming with you.'

Becks stands. 'So am I.'

I put a hand on her arm. 'Not this time, Becks. We came far too close to losing you last time.'

Tommaso quietly intervenes. 'If I might make a suggestion?'

Monsieur nods to him. 'Yes, Tommaso. And I think we can all benefit by listening. Sit down, Joe and Becks.' His tone of gentle authority calms everyone down, and Becks and I do as he asks.

Tommaso takes the mouse and scrolls back to the photo portrait of Dieter von Schwarzberg. 'I … have a contact who may be able to supply some intelligence on this gentleman. His second-in-command had a number of dealings with the Camorra.'

Monsieur glances at Dad. 'You would be well-advised, Julius. This young man's experience makes him a powerful ally, as he has been already.'

'And Mum would be a lot less unhappy if she knew you had us with you, Dad.'

'I don't think she's at all happy about any of this sorry business, Joe. Let's just hope we can get it done as quickly as possible!'

Tommaso and I exchange looks. It's a Yes.

Monsieur gets up. 'I will organise pre-flight checks on the helicopter. I assume that your first port of call will be the prison?'

After our second re-fuelling stop, Dad checks his watch. 'An hour and forty minutes should do it.' We climb back into Monsieur's copter and Tommaso checks the radar while Dad starts the rotors. I watch his hands, tanned from his epic holiday with Mum, as he works the controls. Sometimes I still can't quite believe he's back, after all those long years without him. But it makes me go cold to think of what is pursuing him from his past.

He puts the copter into a power climb and the ground drops away. Above, the cloud ceiling parts in places to show patches of blue. We've come a long way since we took off from the Château L'Étoile while it was still dark. Now, it won't be long before we have the wilderness of Dartmoor below us.

'This von Schwarzberg is German, isn't he Dad?'

'You're right in thinking he should have been in a Berlin jail, not here. But his legal team managed to convince the judiciary to place him in Her Majesty's Prison Dartmoor.'

'Why here and not Berlin?'

Dad looks at me briefly at me before he turns his attention back to the cloud ceiling. 'Britain is the only country in Western Europe that doesn't have armed guards on the prison walls.'

'So he was planning his escape even before he was put away!'

'I had misgivings about it at the time. But there was nothing I could do.'

Tommaso says quietly, 'Criminals like von Schwarzberg have a great deal of influence. It is like where the underworld joins the more respectable overworld.'

'The perfect way of putting it, Tommaso!' We burst out from the clouds into the blue and Dad levels off.

—⁂—

The clouds break up to give glimpses of the wild terrain below us, as we begin the descent. And then we see it, set in those bleak hills. Four-storey buildings radiating from the centre in a star shape, completely encircled by high granite walls. The main gate has a cast-iron bell hanging from it. They must have used to ring it when there was a break-out.

'It looks old.'

'Early eighteen hundreds. There's talk of it being closed in three years. I shouldn't wonder if that decided von Schwarzberg to get out.'

Tommaso comments, 'Because then he could

have been transferred to a German jail where escape would have been far more difficult.'

Dad radios to the prison and we're told we can land on a football pitch inside the grounds. As the rotors slow, a dark-haired middle-aged woman in a smart business suit comes towards us. 'The Governor,' says Dad. 'Mrs Melanie Gibson.' Mrs Gibson shakes hands with all of us, and if she's surprised to see me and Tommaso, she doesn't show it.

We follow her into her office, where she looks appraisingly at Dad. 'You were the undercover agent who got von Schwarzberg put away, Commander Grayling?'

'Correct, and I do appreciate you giving us your time, Mrs Gibson.'

'If we can get this gentleman back where he belongs, that will be well worthwhile. However, I doubt if it will be here. Do be seated, all of you. Coffee? Tea?'

Over coffee, Dad gets straight to the point. 'Can you tell me how extensive the search was – the area it covered?'

'With the whole crew of them escaping by helicopter, we got onto the local RAF command and they scrambled a couple of Eurofighter Typhoons. They did an extensive air search but never picked up a thing.'

'So it's possible that the fugitives landed and took cover somewhere quite local?'

'That's a line of enquiry I would pursue, Commander Grayling. Keep me informed.'

It's late afternoon when we lift off from Dartmoor Prison, but still plenty of light for spotting copters on the ground. As we fly in ever increasing circles across the wild moorland at around five hundred feet, we all munch on the huge supply of sandwiches that Mum's packed, and swig coffee from flasks. Dad looks across to Tommaso who's on the radar. 'What's the next town we're heading for, Tommaso?'

'Moretonhampstead, Uncle.'

'So we should start to see some rural properties quite soon.'

We fly over a series of very large bungalows with acres of wooded ground around them. There are ponies in some of the fields, but no copters. Then we're back over bleak moorland. 'Ashburton is next,' comments Tommaso. Then he exclaims, as we fly over a deep valley, 'Can we take a closer look down there, Uncle?'

We circle round and Dad puts the copter into a slow descent, then into hover. It's only a small cottage, nestling in the depths of the valley. But there's something else nearby. In the lengthening shadows of the surrounding hills, the fading light glints on huge rotors. Tommaso sights through his binoculars. 'A Sikorsky – probably a ten-seater.'

'Plenty of room for von Schwarzberg's little army in that,' says Dad. He passes his phone to me. 'Can you send the co-ordinates to the prison, Joe.'

Tommaso is still training the binoculars on the ground. Suddenly he shouts, 'They are firing Uncle!'

Instantly, Dad wheels the copter, and we power away up the valley sides. Looking down, I can see a flashing, but I can't hear anything because of the noise of the rotors. Dad doesn't pull out of the climb until we're well out of Death Valley. Where they were obviously expecting us.

Sending a warning message to the prison about the warm welcome that greeted us, we fly on towards our next refuelling point.

I'm trying to work out how the escape went. 'So, they could have transferred to cars at the cottage and driven under cover of darkness …'

'To the nearest private airfield. There are a great many on Dartmoor. From there, they probably took a roundabout route to their next stop. Which almost certainly was not in Germany.'

Tommaso says, 'Von Schwarzberg's second-in-command was not based in Berlin.'

'Of course!'

I ask Tommaso, 'So, where is he based, this second-in-command?'

'*She* is based in Antibes, in the South of France.'

'That's a bit close to our place for comfort.'

Dad frowns, 'But there's something else we need to know. Is she still the second-in-command, or has she taken over the show? It often happens when the boss is banged up.'

'Like the Contessa. When she went on the run, Amadeo turned on her.'

'But if that's the case, who master-minded the escape? Can you shed any light on this, Tommaso?'

Tommaso is staring at the radar. 'We are being followed. I think it is the Sikorsky.'

'Damn.' Dad looks at the gauge. 'We could outrun them easily, but I've been trying to stretch the fuel.'

'And I guess they're armed …'

'All we have on our side is the failing light. We still have forty miles to the nearest refuelling stop.'

Tommaso says cautiously, 'I brought something that might help?' Reaching under his seat, he produces one of the laser hand guns from Monsieur's Bentley. 'Let us hope that they do not have a jamming device like Azarov.'

'You star! I'm going to put her down here.' Dad starts a rapid descent towards a bare stretch of moorland, growing increasingly dim in the dusk. Looking up, we can now see the red and green navigation lights of the monstrous Sikorsky looming about five hundred feet above us.

We hit the ground with a bump and Tommaso jumps out, aiming the laser gun at the huge copter's cabin. He fires and a bright pencil beam attaches itself to the copter. There's a flash inside the cabin, and the machine lurches wildly above us.

'You've done it Tommaso! Now let's get the hell out of here!'

Tommaso scrambles back on board and Dad pushes our copter into a full power climb. The monster above starts to make a lumbering emergency landing, all of its communications systems taken out. For a few seconds, it looks as though they're falling straight towards us. Then the two copters pass within around sixty feet of each other, ours going very fast up and theirs coming clumsily down.

Dad switches off our navigation lights until we're out of range of a bullet. Now we're all just holding our breath, hoping that we'll make it to the refuelling point.

A gruelling twelve hours later, having flown through the night and the following morning, Dad radios as we approach the paddocks outside the Château L'Étoile. 'Requesting permission to land?'

'Permission granted. Please, all of you, come straight to my study.' Monsieur's voice has a note of urgency. I wonder if they've had any unwanted visitors in our absence. Part of this question is answered as we begin our descent. Parked in the driveway of the château is a red Lamborghini Gallardo convertible.

CHAPTER 2

A Trick Of The Light

Inside Monsieur's study, a smiling Becks is sitting in a leather armchair next to Monsieur. And from another armchair, Daha stands to greet us as we enter. Instead of the designer jeans and bare feet when we first met him in Surat, the brillianteer is wearing an elegant deep blue suit. The dark, tunnel eyes glow with pleasure as he holds out his hand. 'My dear friends, it is very good to see you again!'

'This is fantastic, Daha!'

Monsieur says, 'Daha has come here at considerable risk to himself, for two reasons. But first, coffee is on the way. Although I doubt it will be of the quality of that which you served as part of your hospitality in Surat, Daha.'

Once everyone has topped up on coffee and caught up on general chat, Daha settles into his armchair and begins his story, addressing himself at first to Becks, Tommaso and me. 'You remember, I am sure, our conversation about the blue diamond pendant. The shocking circumstances of its theft …' He glances respectfully at Monsieur. 'And although you texted me later that Monsieur had instructed you all to pursue it no further because of the danger, the memory of that conversation lived on with me.'

He pauses to take a sip of his coffee. 'We all knew that Amadeo had been arrested and would be put away for a long time. What we didn't know was whether he had disposed of the pendant before his arrest. I was pondering about various ways he could have hidden it, when I received a communication from a lady I used to know before she married. She was, and still is, an Indian princess of great beauty and few scruples. She contacted me because her new husband wanted to make her a gift of a magnificent blue diamond he had acquired. But, she said, he wanted it re-cut and reset first.'

'To disguise its provenance?'

'There is rarely any other reason, Joe. Which was confirmed when she sent me a photo.' He scrolls through files on his phone. And suddenly the iridescence of blue and violet glows from the screen.

Becks draws in her breath. 'The setting's the same!'

I glance towards Monsieur. He's looking at Daha with an expression of concern. 'Go on, Daha. What was your response?'

The dark eyes gaze directly at Monsieur. 'I asked her to send the diamond to me and told her how this must happen. A very secure route, of course.'

'So you agreed to re-cut it?'

Daha smiles at Becks. 'I agreed to look at it.' He

slips his hand into his pocket and opens his palm. The blue fire hits our eyes. 'And now, you are all looking at it.'

He holds the flashing pendant in long, delicate fingers. 'What was once a blood diamond can once again become a love diamond.' Standing, with a slight bow, the young double agent hands the pendant to Monsieur.

Monsieur stands to take the pendant and gazes at the jewel he has not seen for more than seventeen years: the jewel that his beloved wife was wearing the last time he saw her alive. His brow is still furrowed with concern. 'You have given me back a part of my life that I thought was lost forever, Daha; I can never thank you enough. But I hope you have not endangered your own life in doing this?'

Daha shrugs. 'This Indian princess of few scruples would not have dreamed of checking the credentials of the stone I sent to her, re-cut and in its brand new setting. And with my bill, of course. Reassuringly expensive. That always boosts credibility.'

Becks asks what I've been thinking. 'Was it the fake blue diamond that you re-cut and reset, Daha?'

Daha smiles. 'What fake was that, Becks?'

And I remember his words, back in Surat, as we gazed on the depths of blue and purple: ... *a fake diamond can shed just as much light as a real one.*

Before we move on to the second reason for Daha's visit, Monsieur insists that we all eat, which everyone is very glad to do. Over the meal, Dad brings everyone up-to-date with the Dartmoor expedition and our friendly welcome when we found the Sikorsky.

Monsieur nods. 'And after lunch, you will find that there is an interesting convergence between your pursuit of von Schwarzberg and the intelligence that Daha brings.'

Back in Monsieur's study, Daha slips his hand into his other pocket and produces a small packet of white powder. 'Heroin. And not just addictive. This stuff is lethal.'

He looks at Dad. 'As you know, Commander Grayling, there is a narcotics epidemic in Germany. The heroin manufactured by von Schwarzberg's crew, and the shiploads of cocaine coming in from Colombia. But it has become even worse. Once Von Schwarzberg's operation was shut down, predictably, others were quick to take its place. And now we are seeing an influx of heroin cut with all kinds of hugely dangerous chemicals.' He spreads his hands in a gesture of despair. 'The epidemic has become mass murder – something has to be done!'

'We never caught von Schwarzberg's second-in-command …'

'We do suspect her, Commander. We think she has set up a clandestine narcotics laboratory and is continuing to supply what was von Schwarzberg's market.'

'Daha, are you thinking that this is why von Schwarzberg chose now to escape?'

'He would be aware that his second-in-command seems to have moved in on his empire, Joe. He would not like that.'

'What's this woman like, Daha?'

'Gerda Budd got to be second-in-command by her ability to organise with military precision. You would know that, Tommaso?'

With a slight smile, Tommaso nods. 'Oh yes. She was not in the least afraid during her dealings with the Camorra. Although perhaps she should have been.'

Daha slips the deadly little packet back into his pocket. 'But the biggest question mark in all this is von Schwarzberg.'

Dad looks at his nephew. 'Did you say you had a contact who might be able to supply some intelligence, Tommaso?'

'Yes, Uncle. And he has. I now have von Schwarzberg's mobile number.'

'Excellent!' Monsieur explains to Daha, 'Tommaso could hack into the Kremlin.'

'Perhaps he should,' comments Daha, 'And now I have to be on my way. Thank you for your hospitality, Monsieur le Comte …'

Monsieur shakes his hand warmly, 'I owe you a great debt, Daha.'

Daha gives another gracious bow. 'No, Monsieur. What was yours has been returned. But will you please keep me informed of developments? And if I can help in any way …?' A few moments later, the snarl of the Lambo's V10 engine recedes down the drive.

The following evening we're all sat round Tommaso's laptop as he shows us the results of a quite spectacular hack. 'First, there are the sent and received text messages, with none received from Gerda Budd. So it would seem that she was not involved in the jailbreak of her former boss.'

'Indicating that she is now operating in competition with anything von Schwarzberg may wish to set up.'

Tommaso's voice is cautious. 'That could be the case, Uncle. Instead, there are regular exchanges with someone who is referred to as Lo Coltello – Italian for The Knife. This man is probably the most dangerous Camorristo alive today.'

'So it was the Camorra who got von Schwarzberg out?'

'It would seem so, Becks.'

Dad frowns. 'Looks like some kind of unholy alliance is being formed.'

'Have you been able to pinpoint von Schwarzberg's movements, Tommaso? Do we know where he is now?'

'We know where he was last night, Monsieur. He now has his phone switched off.'

Becks stares at the text messages on the laptop. 'But last night?'

'Last night, von Schwarzkopf was in Antibes. These were the co-ordinates.' Tommaso clicks on a file and the co-ordinates flash onto the screen.

Becks stares at them. 'Antibes. Where this woman runs her factory?'

'We don't know that the factory's there. But it's where she apparently lives.'

'Can we look at the precise location?'

Google Earth reveals a white-walled villa with Mediterranean blue shutters and a swimming pool. 'Nice,' comments Becks.

Dad asks, 'Any further shots, Tommaso? It would be good to know how extensive the grounds are. She could have an underground factory.'

'There are no other photos, Uncle.'

'So, a night mission for the Velociraptor?'

Tommaso shakes his head. 'I don't think you should go anywhere near this place, Uncle. I think it's a trap.'

This isn't the first time that Tommaso has taken my breath away, but I still haven't got used to his rapier-sharp brain. And all that dark intelligence that he gathered during his time in the Camorra. I glance at Monsieur and I can see that he agrees with the young Camorristo.

Tommaso continues, 'It was too easy to hack von Schwarzberg's phone. His first aim is still to take revenge on you, Uncle. So he is luring you to Antibes, where Lo Coltello has been instructed to kill you.'

There's total silence in Monsieur's study. Then

Dad says quietly, 'Point taken, Tommaso. What do you suggest we do?'

'You are right about unholy alliances, Uncle. Not only is von Schwarzberg's second-in-command dealing with the Camorra, but so is he.'

Becks says, 'So, this drug smuggling scene could be all joined up?'

'Organised crime has become like a global corporation, Becks. In many countries, it is rooted in governments – or is controlling them.' Tommaso turns to Monsieur. 'You know, when you said I was capable of hacking into the Kremlin, Monsieur – and Daha said perhaps I should …?'

Monsieur says softly, 'He was not joking, was he?'

'No, Monsieur. We all know that drugs trafficking pays for illegal arms and international terrorism. The Kremlin has long been an accomplice of terrorism around the world.'

My brain is now working at slightly above crawling pace. 'So the Alyona, that ship loaded with cruise missiles …'

Monsieur adds, 'The Kremlin would have had full knowledge of Azarov's little expedition. So would the Camorra. In the same way that thousands of illegal arms made in Russia find their way to terrorist groups, they are also traded to the likes of the Camorra and von Schwarzberg. Usually in return for narcotics – von Schwarzberg's speciality.'

Becks fixes Tommaso's blue eyes with her own

green ones. 'So it's all like one big smooth machine. And are you suggesting we do something they are not expecting, Tommaso?'

'We disrupt this smooth machine. We want von Schwarzberg to become suspicious of his new partners. Then he will start to make mistakes. And then – we bring him down.' I stare at Tommaso. These are the words of a seasoned spymaster who's learned his craft in the most deadly school in the world.

Dad is looking at his young nephew with new eyes. 'So if we can, say, put a spoke in their supply chain? There must be a steady stream of ships like the Alyona coming out of Russia, round the Arctic Circle and heading for trouble spots all over the world.'

Monsieur gets up. 'We need to contact Icebreaker, Zeitgeist and Le Loup. Each of them could have intelligence that may help us get this man back into custody.'

'From what Daha has told us,' says Dad, 'we need to try and shut down Gerda Budd's operation as well.'

'D'accord. Once we have the intelligence, I will pass it on to the Marseille Chief of Police.'

'We can also ensure that von Schwarzberg receives information that convinces him I'm being an obliging puppet on a string.' Dad heads for his study.

'Tommaso, can I ask a big favour?'
'What is that, Becks?'

'Can I watch you hack the Kremlin, please? I consider it a vital part of my education.'

It's after lunch the next day when Becks and I sit down with Tommaso in Monsieur's study. The alarm and defence systems are still on, but we can monitor them all from here. Tommaso is online, tapping into his laptop. 'Hacking is about finding vulnerabilities. For this vulnerability in a particular Windows protocol, Microsoft eventually provided a patch – that is, a fix. But not all machines in Russia were patched.'

'Why not? Surely if a patch is available, you'd want to use it.'

'You would be surprised how complacent people can be, Becks. They have no idea that every minute of every day and night, people like me are prowling the web, looking for weaknesses in their machines.'

'But Moscow is one of the world's most powerful cyber forces, isn't it?'

Tommaso's blue eyes are on the screen. 'Most powerful means they can cause the most harm, Joe. And they do. But it doesn't mean that they are the most intelligent.'

'Are you saying that the Kremlin has machines that aren't patched for these vulnerabilities?'

Tommaso gives his slight smile. 'Sometimes, they have software so old, that a patch is not even available. That is what I am looking at here.'

Becks leans forward to look at the screen. 'So, what are you doing?'

'I am looking to take over this machine as an administrator – like a prison inmate who has stolen the warden's keys.'

'So – you don't want to get spotted!'

'Definitely not, Becks.'

'How are you going to avoid that?'

'Sometimes the Russian government is its own worst enemy. So, they allow the military to have the latest Microsoft operating system. But the top man, and those closest to him, are stuck with old stuff with little or no protection. Like this!'

He hits a key and suddenly the almost blank screen, with its bald list of instructions, changes. We're into someone's email. Tommaso nods and hits another key. 'It is all in Russian. I am sending it to Icebreaker to translate.'

'And this guy in the Kremlin won't notice what you've done?'

Tommaso's fingers blur over the keyboard. 'Only if I want him to. Plenty of hackers like their victims to know what has happened to them. But they are stupid – it gives them away.'

He clicks on Send from his email. 'And now, Icebreaker has it.' He gets up. 'Tomorrow, I am hopeful that he will have some news for us about Russian ships sailing from the Arctic Circle.'

After Tommaso has left the study, Becks says quietly, 'Can we take a walk in the grounds? I could do with some fresh air.'

Drops of rain are falling lightly as we stroll down the woodland walk. With a fluttering of dark wings, Corbo alights on a branch up ahead of us and preens his shiny feathers.

'I ... think I know what's on your mind, Becks.'

'Then here goes. On the Bristol suspension bridge, a week ago, you said that there was so much of your dad's past that you knew absolutely nothing about. How much more is there to come, Joe?'

'That's what I'm wondering.'

'And your mum. This must be horrible for her!'

I'm silent for a few moments. Then I tell Becks what I've been thinking for an awfully long time. 'I love Dad. I'll always love him. But there is a darkness about him. All that time when he never told anyone about his brother Sebastian, Tommaso's father.'

Becks murmurs, 'And all that time when he never came home.'

I look up at the raven. He takes flight down the length of the walk and disappears. 'I mean ... there's loads we don't know about Monsieur, too. But now that justice has been done as far as it can be, surely there's nothing in his past that could hurt people?'

'How much do you think Monsieur knows about your dad's past? They did work together once, didn't they?'

'They must have been in life or death situations together; but Monsieur never knew about Dad's brother … And in the time since they last worked together, a lot could have happened.'

―⁂―

We meet up again with Tommaso in the study after breakfast the next day. 'Icebreaker has had no trouble translating the emails. But he tells me that they seem to be using some kind of code to communicate shipping movements.' Tommaso scrolls down. 'Here, for example. *The white bird flies south on the fourth day.*'

Becks googles 'white birds of Russia' on her phone. 'The Arctic tern is almost all white – just has a black head and wingtips. It says they begin their migration southward from the Arctic in August.'

'And look at this!' I've found another website. 'Some Arctic terns fly to the Cape of Good Hope via West Africa – there are any number of trouble hotspots in Africa that would welcome illegal arms shipments from Russia!'

Becks glances back to Tommaso's screen. 'So, we're looking at the 4th August for the sailing?'

'That's four weeks away.'

Tommaso has now found another website. 'If what they are referring to is the Arctic tern, it has the longest migration of any bird. Twenty-five thousand miles, from the Arctic to the Antarctic and back again. That could be telling us two important things.'

'Nuclear-powered, like the Alyona?'

'Definitely, Joe.'

'And there could be a number of drops on a route that long? Not just Africa but South America too?'

'And pickups, Becks. Much of the world's cocaine supply comes from South America – Colombia most of all.'

'So, where would be the best place to disrupt the machine?'

'We could begin with the narcotics entering Europe. There is a great deal of Camorra activity in Napoli container port – but that place has become too dangerous for all of us now, after Amadeo was arrested. Another hotspot is Marseille.'

My eyes are out on stalks. 'When you say container port – you mean they stuff whole containers full of narcotics?'

He goes on Google and brings up an article from the Wall Street Journal. 'It is quite common. After all, with more 700 million 20-foot containers being shipped around the world each year, how can you possibly check them all? But they got this one!'

Becks and I stare at the article. It's headed '*Inside Shipping's Record Cocaine Bust*'. Becks exclaims, 'The numbers are eye-watering! US Customs officials seized nearly *twenty tons* of cocaine with a street value of *1.3 billion dollars* in seven shipping containers.'

Tommaso brings up another document, this time from the United Nations Container Control Program. 'The numbers are more than any port authority can hope to deal with. If the world's shipping containers were positioned end to end, they would reach to the moon and back five times! Most consumer goods travel to us in this way.'

'So – where do we come in, Tommaso?'

He closes down the web pages. 'It is up to the port authorities to do their best with the containers. That is far too big for us to try and disrupt. But the Camorra have also adopted a different technique. They attach the drugs to the bottom of the container ship. I think that here, we can cause them some annoyance. But first, we have to persuade your father that he must not be part of this.'

'You're the only one who can do that, Tommaso!'

—⁂—

'As soon as you are out of those gates, Uncle, they will be after you. You will be doing exactly what they want. What they will not expect is for you to run a campaign of disinformation from here. Without that we have no hope of success.'

Dad is silent. This goes against all his instincts. But he's still listening to his young Camorristo nephew.

'So we need to set up a dedicated computer posing as yours, Dad. Not networked to the others and not too easy to hack. But vulnerable.'

Becks joins in. 'I'll help put together a stack of files with fake plans and contacts.'

'And you will need a new phone, Uncle. Because I will be taking yours with me to Antibes, by way of

Marseille. They will follow it on satnav and believe that you have taken the bait.'

Dad shakes his head. 'No, you're not doing decoy, Tommaso. I won't let you put yourself in harm's way like that.'

'They will not be expecting me, Uncle. They will be on the lookout for you. And Lo Coltello doesn't know me. I was a very small cog in the machine with the Camorra.'

Dad is still unconvinced. 'And – by way of Marseille?'

Tommaso's blue eyes look at Dad straight on. 'I know a guy who works in the container port. He will be able to inform me about the Camorra's cocaine smuggling activities there.'

And now Dad is looking straight back. 'Because presumably, he's part of it?'

Tommaso doesn't blink. 'So was I, Uncle. Which reminds me, Joe. Can you scuba dive?'

'Nope. But I'd love to learn!'

Monsieur says, 'We have scuba gear. We will use the outdoor pool.'

That's when we all look at Becks. She's been expecting this. 'Y'know what, guys? I have a law exam coming up that I want to get top marks in. So is it OK if I take a break from swimming for a while?'

I give her a potentially rib-breaking hug. 'I am so glad you said that, Becks!'

She smiles back. 'One day, when I'm a star prosecuting lawyer, you'll all be glad!'

CHAPTER 3

Dive

So while Tommaso starts to lay a trail to deceive the enemy, through the Marseille container port and then onwards to Antibes, Monsieur teaches me scuba. His outdoor pool is perfect, because in addition to the main swimming area, it has a diving pool that is six metres deep. I've dived off the ten metre board a few times. It's nothing like as terrifying as when Becks and I jumped off the Alyona into the whirlpool; but you still appreciate that depth when you hit the water like a ballistic missile.

Before I get anywhere near the pool, Monsieur gives me theory lessons that are a crash course in real, practical Physics that can prevent you from dying. Like, what happens to your body the deeper you get underwater. Why, at depth, you absolutely must not surface too fast. How long an oxygen tank will last at given depths. How to check your equipment. Then, there are the hand signals. Because you can't just phone your mate and tell him there's a Great White behind him.

Next day, while Becks and Dad are hard at work putting together a load of fake information on the new computer and digging a few holes in its firewall, Monsieur and I drive to Aix-en-Provence rail station to pick up Tommaso. Over lunch, he tells us all how it went. 'I switched off the phone in Antibes, not far from Gerda Budd's villa. So they should now believe that you, Uncle, have travelled there and are somewhere in the vicinity.'

Becks adds, 'I've been busy sending fake emails to the rogue computer, to support your dad's itinerary, Joe.'

Dad taps his tablet, showing a file directory. 'And we're being supersmart. I'm putting genuine files, which are no more use to us, in among the fake ones. That way, each directory looks pretty solid.'

Monsieur looks at me and Tommaso. 'Right, allowing an hour to digest your lunch, we will meet at the pool and put you both through your paces underwater. And I have some essential equipment for you.'

Tommaso's performance underwater convinces me that he's got plenty of previous. He's a powerful and experienced diver and he gives me a lot of help. And my slow brain is beginning to connect the idea of scuba diving with drugs attached to the bottom of container ships. Well, I'd guessed this was no holiday on the Great Barrier Reef.

When we surface after the fifteenth dive, Monsieur nods us out. He's holding two techy looking diving watches. 'Each is fitted with a tracker.

You are going into a situation where I need to know exactly where you are, because the worst could happen.' He hands the watches over and picks up the tracker unit. 'We will check that all is working well – in you go!'

Watches strapped on, Tommaso and I dive right to the bottom of the pool. We hold there until he gives us the thumbs up, then we rise gently. As we break water, Monsieur is nodding approvingly. 'The signal is strong, and it will need to be.'

'How far below the surface could this container's bottom be, Tommaso?'

'Maybe ten metres.'

'Quite a bit deeper than this pool, Joe. And you will have a long swim to the container ship. But I think you now have the basics. You just need to follow Tommaso as your dive leader.'

Once we're dry and drinking coffee in Monsieur's office, I ask, 'How do they attach the drugs to the bottom of these container ships?'

'Some use suction cups, others powerful magnets.' Monsieur pulls up some images. 'The drugs are contained in nets, which the divers cut, throw the drugs into speedboats and they're gone.'

'And they do this while the ship is in port?'

'Normally they would, Joe. Because they have contacts in the port authorities who they bribe or blackmail not to notice. But we cannot afford to wait until the ship is in port. Too much competition!'

Monsieur explains: 'With all these vast numbers of container ships waiting to enter port, there are queues. Tommaso has obtained information about a ship, loaded with hull-mounted drugs, that will be waiting to enter Marseille container port from tomorrow around 17.00 hours.'

'How long will they have to wait?'

'That is what we can only guess at.'

The following day at twelve, Tommaso and I are in the Bentley with our dive gear and Monsieur is driving rapidly towards Marseille.

Marseille Old Port is bustling with yachts coming in to moorings or casting off, as we walk along the pontoon towards the Lisette. Her graceful 60-foot white hull moves gently on the water as we slip on board. Monsieur does a final check on the weather forecast. 'Wind Force 4 rising to 5. Falling later.' He starts the engine and Tommaso and I cast off at the stern and prow and jump onto the deck. The yacht starts to move away from her mooring.

A few minutes later, we're passing the harbour walls and the lighthouse. I take the wheel while Monsieur cuts the engine and hoists the jib, followed by the mighty mainsail. He returns to the wheel and Tommaso and I take up lookout posts fore and aft. With a Slap, the main fills up with wind. The sun is drifting towards the sea and the wind is rising as we sail towards the horizon.

Twenty minutes later, Tommaso calls, 'I can see a ship!' Joining him at the prow as he sights through his binoculars, I can pick out the squat silhouette of a container ship where the sky meets the sea. Behind it, maybe a mile distant, is another ship. We've reached the queue.

We continue sailing in a wide arc around the ship until we're on its port side. It's fifteen minutes past five. Monsieur is comparing our position with the co-ordinates Tommaso has given him. 'It is the first ship: the Everglade.'

Tommaso and I check our diving watches then strap on our oxygen cylinders, flippers and head torches. We get into position on the side of the yacht that any lookout on the Everglade won't be able to see. Monsieur turns the Lisette into the wind so that she stops, sails flapping – 'Good luck and take care!' Then we're rolling off the side and tumbling neatly into the water.

We dive immediately to avoid being spotted. Above us, Monsieur is turning the Lisette so that the sails once more fill with air. We've got one hour to get to the ship, remove and dump the drugs and get back to the yacht: any longer than that, and our tanks will be getting dangerously low. Monsieur will be watching our tracking signals every second of that time.

From time to time we surface, to see the vast hull of the monster looming ever larger. As the sun drops lower, giving us a cloak of invisibility, lights start to twinkle on the ship. And now we're just a few feet from a vessel that's as tall as a tower block. Layer upon layer of 20-foot containers are towering two hundred feet above us, as many above deck as there are below. We must look like tiny shrimps, way down here in the water.

Tommaso gives me the signal and the shrimps dive. Down and down, bubbles streaming upwards. Bubbles going off in my head as we dive deeper and deeper. Head torches carving through the thickening gloom. Now we're ten metres underwater and this huge darkness above is the ship. It's like being on Earth, looking up at a monster spaceship that's just over your head.

We start swimming the 300 metres towards the stern. The head torches shine on the ship's bottom, pimpled with barnacles and growths of sea plants. I glance at my watch. Forty minutes left. Tommaso nods and we kick on harder, faster. If the drugs cache is attached near the propellers, we've got to swim the entire length of the ship – that's the same as six 50 metre lengths in an Olympic-size swimming pool. At least we have flippers to turbocharge our feet.

We're getting uncomfortably close to the enormous propellers, when Tommaso touches my arm and points upwards. There's something bulbous attached to the hull ahead of us. As we get closer it's obvious that this is what we've been looking for. The net is around twenty by twenty feet, attached to the hull by magnets. It's packed with bales the size of suitcases, encased in layers of bubble wrap. Twenty five minutes left.

Tommaso whips a knife out of the leg of his

wetsuit and slashes through the net. The bales of cocaine tumble out. There must be a hundred of them. But they don't sink; they just float off towards Marseille. I have a fleeting vision of them washing up in Marseille harbour, right under the noses of the customs officials.

Twenty minutes to go. We head out from under the shadow of this monstrous ship and start to swim back out towards the Lisette's position. As we swim, very gradually we start to move upwards towards the surface.

We have five minutes before we need to reach the Lisette, when I see the beginnings of the underside of a hull and a keel ahead. It's not the Lisette: it's a black hull and not a 60-footer. Looks more like a large speedboat.

Tommaso has seen it too. He's making urgent signals for us to get the hell out, when four divers approach from behind us. Two of them have vicious looking knives. By sheer bad luck we've bumped into a band of shoppers who've had exactly the same idea as us. They must have been less than happy when they realised the shelves were empty.

As we're dragged into the motor launch, I quickly look around in the evening light for the Lisette. No sign of her. Monsieur must have seen this crew coming and guessed their mission. Seconds later, I can't see anything because after cuffing us hand

and foot, they blindfold us. There's a lot of talk in rapid-fire Italian, which Tommaso can understand. But at least they're not beating us up or worse for sabotaging their cocaine haul. Not yet, anyway.

With a roar, the powerful marine diesel fires up and the launch takes off. Manacled hand and foot, I sway around on my seat as we race along, spray flying in my face. Where the hell are we going? They must know that someone dropped us off for the dive. But hopefully, they'll assume it was a speedboat, not a 60-foot sailing yacht. And with the speed we're doing, the Lisette will never be in sight of them.

After around twenty minutes, the thunder of the engine drops to a booming. We must be entering Marseille Old Port to tie up. I bet they wouldn't be here if they'd had the drugs on board. It must be night as our feet are uncuffed and we're dragged out of the boat and onto the pontoon. So there's no one around to see two blindfolded prisoners being pushed along the harbourside and bundled into the rear of a van, where we sit on the floor.

We drive for about five minutes before the van stops. More pushing and shoving and a door opens on squeaking hinges. The space we enter echoes our footsteps; maybe it's an old warehouse. Then I'm thrust onto a chair and lashed to it, still blindfolded. There are more mutterings in Italian before a light switch clicks, the door bangs shut and a key turns in the lock. An engine revs and fades. Then, silence. It feels pretty certain that we're waiting for someone.

A Someone who is not happy about us spoiling his plans. A Someone who has as a sidekick the most deadly Camorristo of all.

—⚋—

Tommaso remains silent and I follow his lead. The place could be bugged. They probably bring kidnap victims here on a regular basis and I can guess what for. I test the tightness of the ropes tying me to the chair. No chance, they're cutting off my circulation. I have two consolations though. One is the snug feel of the tracker watch around my wrist: because even if they take the watches off us now, Monsieur has the co-ordinates of where we are. The other is relief that Becks is safe at L'Ētoile.

I've lost all sense of time, when a key turns in the lock, a light switch clicks, footsteps approach and the blindfolds are ripped off our heads. At first, I can't see anything: a spotlight is shining straight at us. Behind it, in the shadows, a man is seating himself at a table, observing us. He seems to be wearing glasses; I can't tell if he's balding or not. Behind him, in deeper shadow, stands another man.

In impeccable English, von Schwarzberg says quietly, 'What a pity your father did not have the guts to come on this mission himself, Joe Grayling. It would have saved us all a great deal of time and trouble. However, you can make up for it now by simply telling us where he is.'

Neither of us says anything. Von Schwarzberg

gets up from behind the desk and saunters towards us. A movement in the shadows tells us that The Knife could be getting restless. 'You really need to stop wasting our time and talk, my young friends. It's useless to try and protect this man. Do you know how many deaths he has on his hands?'

'A fraction of the number you've got!'

His face tightens. 'I have never killed anyone in my life!'

'Nah, you just pay other people to do your dirty work.'

Lo Coltello moves slowly towards the lamplight. Behind his shades I'm sure his eyes are directed towards Tommaso. Is he thinking back, dredging his memory? If he clocks that Tommaso used to work for the Camorra, it's going to be the end of the road for both of us.

I have to create a diversion. 'You've got a new hitman now, haven't you? That dude behind you. Has he got a skin complaint that he avoids standing in the light? Or perhaps he's a vampire?' My barrage of insults seems to stun the pair of them. But at least the Camorristo is looking at me now, not Tommaso. So I go on. 'He and his mates got you out of prison, didn't they? So you must owe them big time, now. What's the price of your freedom, Dieter?'

With a lightning swiftness, the man they call The Knife explodes out of the shadows and kicks our chairs over. As my head hits the floor, the cold edge of a blade is at my throat. Von Schwarzberg stands over us. 'My friend is a man of few words.

But you can take it that the price of *your* freedom, Joe Grayling, will be your father's.'

They've gone, leaving us in the dark, lying on our backs still tied to the chairs. Tommaso whispers, 'I still have my knife in the leg of my wetsuit.' There then follows a wrestling match with our chairs that would be comical if it wasn't such a dire situation.

With a great deal of shoving and swearing, I get my chair lined up with my back to Tommaso, and between us we get the knife out of the wetsuit. Then he starts sawing away at my ropes. And finally, we're both free. He switches on the desk light and we look around. I whisper, 'Do you think they'll be back soon?'

'They will probably leave it a few hours, to soften us up. Now, we need to check for cameras.' They haven't bothered to conceal the two cameras fitted in this windowless hulk of a building. One of them is aimed at the door.

'So, if we switch off the light …' At that moment there's a loud bang and the light goes out all by itself. Seconds later, we can smell smoke. 'It must be an electrical fault. Quick, Joe – the head torches!'

We shine the torches round the walls. Mine picks out a fuse box with flames crackling out of it and its door hanging on one hinge. Wildly we look around for something to extinguish the fire. There's another explosion from the fuse box and a flying spark lands on a pile of old newspapers. In seconds they're blazing.

Coughing, we grope our way towards the door, Tommaso with knife in hand to try and pick the lock. But the door is opening without any help from us. Frozen, we watch. If our captors are back again, this is going to end badly.

With a powerful torch, Monsieur guides us out of the burning building and into the waiting Bentley. He takes a circuitous route through the twisting back streets of Marseille to throw any pursuers off the scent.

An hour later, the wrought iron gates of L'Ētoile swing silently open, and the gleaming cats eyes light us up the driveway. In the light of the porch, the sixteen point star carved into the oak door glints softly. I have never been so glad to come home.

CHAPTER 4

Mikes, Cameras, Action!

At breakfast the next morning, we don't mention our narrow escape. I don't want to worry Mum, just when she's looking less stressed, and getting involved with Dad and Becks in the disinformation project. The three of them finish breakfast quickly, and go off to Dad's study, which has been rebranded 'The Ops Room'. Becks teases Dad that it would be better called 'The Apps Room'.

I help myself to another pain au chocolat, while Monsieur pours more coffee and Tommaso finishes his ham and eggs. 'So, the cocaine that we sent for a swim, that was von Schwarzberg's? Or was he planning to nick it from someone else?'

'Probably the latter, Joe.'

Tommaso says, 'My contact in the container port said it was from Colombia. That was all he would say.'

'But von Schwarzberg used to make his own stuff, didn't he?'

'Setting up a drugs manufacturing operation takes time. Unless, of course, he is planning to take over that of his former second-in-command. What is your view Tommaso?'

'If I was Gerda Budd, I would be concerned that von Schwarzberg was planning exactly that.'

'If only we knew where she makes the heroin.' Then I have a lightbulb moment. 'Hey, Tommaso, remember when Zeitgeist offered us some lessons in covert surveillance?'

'And I felt at the time that it was far too soon after your brush with death in the Atlantic,' Monsieur comments.

'We all thought that, Monsieur. But suppose we could enlist Zeitgeist to show us how to watch Gerda Budd's place? That way we could find out if she does have an underground lab, like Dad thought she might?'

'It should be possible to do the surveillance from here. I will talk to Zeitgeist.'

The powerful black agent with the silver hair doesn't hang around. Twenty four hours later, he's installed a camera in a pine tree overlooking the front door and driveway of Gerda Budd's villa. The eye in the tree is movement-activated to conserve battery power, and it has infra-red night vision. As soon as it's activated, it'll stream live footage to us here.

Now it's over to us to watch, 24/7. At the moment, we don't know if the place is inhabited or not. Although the black Merc coupe parked in the driveway says that it very likely is.

We take it in turns, watching in four hour shifts,

in pairs. Day turns into night, and still the eye in the tree tells us nothing. It's three in the morning, and Becks and I are taking over from Dad and Tommaso when we all see the screen flicker into life. The front door of the villa is opening. A shadowy figure with short, curly grey hair wearing a black coat slips out and heads for the Merc.

'That's her,' says Dad. 'Quick, tell Zeitgeist the way is clear.' Gerda Budd gets into the Merc and it glides out of sight of the camera, towards the gates. 'Zeitgeist said he considered trying to bug the car but decided not to chance it with the security system.'

Tommaso uses just one code word in his call to Zeitgeist, pre-agreed with everyone. 'Affirmative'. Now, we have no idea how long Zeitgeist has got before the drugs baroness comes back. And he has a lot to do, this man who once saved us from being buried alive in Napoli. Starting with a break-in.

Next, he has to avoid the movement sensors which are undoubtedly part of Gerda Budd's security system. Then he has to plant voice-activated microphones and movement-activated cameras wherever he thinks they're going to work best. And he has to get out without leaving any trace before she returns. No pressure then.

Monsieur joins us and we all sit round the screen in a tense silence. She might just have popped out to buy a sandwich from an all-night filling station. If so, the black Merc will be coming back up the drive any time soon. And I bet she carries a gun;

which the network agents don't. They rely on their wits; except when they're using firepower to create avalanches of boulders that stop bad men in their tracks, like Zeitgeist did with Amadeo not long ago.

It's gone five in the morning when Tommaso's ring tone makes me jump. He listens, then puts the phone down, saying the second code word: 'Confirmative'. Which means that Zeitgeist's pulled it off – we now have eyes and ears inside this white-walled villa in Antibes.

'Right,' says Dad. 'Over to you, Joe and Becks. It's time Tommaso got some shut-eye.'

The woman who sells drugs that kill people doesn't come back on our watch. It's nine in the morning and I'm trying to stifle one yawn after another, when Dad comes in. 'Anything to report?'

'The outside camera didn't activate once, Dad.'

'So off you go and have some breakfast, then catch up on some sleep.'

'I think I'll sleep first and breakfast at lunchtime.' Becks rubs her eyes. 'I had no idea that surveillance was so nerve-wracking.'

After breakfast, three hours sleep and a swim in the outdoor pool, I feel like I've rejoined the human race. Returning to Monsieur's study, I find Becks munching on a bacon sandwich and Dad frowning at the screen.

The two-way split shows the front door on the left and on the right, a lavish looking living room with marble floor tiles and settees piled high with satin cushions. Gerda Budd is sitting at a desk with her laptop. She's a stocky woman in a white designer trouser suit that's too small for her.

Dad looks round. 'She came back just now. But why are we still getting shots of the front door? There must be something the camera's picking up – but where?'

Tommaso comes in, laptop in hand, and instantly registers the split screen. 'There could be someone other than Zeitgeist who is intending to break in, Uncle.' The outside camera de-activates and we're back to full screen sitting room.

'Someone sent by our German friend, perhaps?'

'Perhaps.'

We watch as Budd closes her laptop and leaves the room. She's caught by the camera in the hall, but then it loses her. The screen goes blank and stays that way.

'So she's not going outside,' muses Dad. 'Oh, by the way, Zeitgeist called to say that he's fitted a tracker to the Merc, inside one of the wheel arches.'

'Brilliant.' Becks pops the remains of her sandwich into her mouth. 'Who's up next?'

'Monsieur and me. I will tell him about the outside camera.' Tommaso opens his laptop and starts to type.

Dad gets up. 'I'm off for some breakfast. Your bacon sandwich has started my stomach rumbling Becks!' He heads for the dining room.

'And I'm off to get on with my revision for that law exam.'

'I suppose I'd better start on my Italian. Library?'

'No, you always natter too much when we revise together. I'm going up to my room.'

'Alright, Miss Goody – I'll bring you a coffee at eleven.'

Going out, we pass Monsieur coming in. He smiles, 'Good luck with the revision,' then seats himself beside Tommaso. The screen is still blank.

In my room, I get through one page of my Italian Revision Guide before I must have dozed off. When I wake up, head on desk, it's five to eleven. After a race to the kitchen, two coffees and me arrive in Becks' room at three minutes past eleven. She looks up from her laptop. 'What sort of time d'you call this?' Shakes her head. 'Can't get the staff!'

Coffee in hand, I go through the stained glass French windows onto her balcony. Below, a fountain of golden stone flashes trickling water in the sunlight. Corbo floats down and stoops to drink. 'Tommaso's pretty sure that von Schwarzberg's going to make a move on Gerda Budd's operation.'

Becks takes a sip of her coffee. 'He's so good at getting into the enemy's head …'

'So if that outside camera did pick up someone staking out her villa …'

'We'd better be right on the case when it's our

watch. See you at one in Monsieur's study!'

Going back to the Italian, this time I do a shedload. Feeling smug, I rendezvous with Becks in the study at five to one. Monsieur looks round. 'She has not gone out – at least, not through the front door to her car. Neither has she returned to the hall or the sitting room. Tommaso feels that there could be an interesting explanation for this.'

'Uncle thought that she could have an underground laboratory. I think he is right. That is where she is now, with her chemist.'

'So this lab is like, right under her house?'

'There are many criminals who operate in underground bunkers, Joe. In Southern Italy, where Mafia bosses run everything, there are hundreds of bunkers.'

'So, what do we do now?'

'Watch, listen and wait. And the disinformation campaign will continue.' Monsieur stands. 'Come, Tommaso, you have earned a good lunch.'

—⁂—

As Becks and I sit down in front of the blank screen, a thought is nagging away that is nothing to do with Gerda Budd. 'The 4th August, when this ship sails from Russia …'

Becks finishes my sentence, 'Is now just two weeks away. You're wondering how long this covert surveillance is going to go on?'

'Well, yeah. But also, we haven't got the tiniest

glimmer of a plan …' My words tail off as the screen flashes on. In broad daylight, two figures wearing black jeans and pullovers, heavy shades and holsters with handguns stride up to Gerda Budd's front door. They don't bother to pick the lock, they just kick the door down. All hell breaks loose as the burglar alarms go off. The hall camera catches them as they barge inside, then they're off camera.

'I'll get Tommaso!' But Tommaso has heard the clamour from the dining room and we almost collide in the doorway. Monsieur and Dad follow. Becks replays the footage.

Tommaso says, 'The taller man is Lo Coltello.'

Becks' voice is very quiet. 'They … they're not going to kill Gerda Budd and her chemist, are they?'

'Normally it is kidnap, Becks.' He doesn't say what could happen after the kidnap. The alarms are still shrieking but the screen is blank. 'Von Schwarzberg will have told them how to get into the bunker.'

'Surely the neighbours will hear the alarms and call the police?'

'In a wealthy neighbourhood like this, people don't want to get involved.'

In silence, we wait for the screen to come alive again. It feels like an age, but it can't have been more than five minutes later when the hall camera catches them. Gerda Budd and a young man in a white lab coat are cuffed and gagged. Their captors are pushing guns into their backs and marching them through the hall and over the remains of the door.

Then something happens that makes us all catch our breath. While The Knife's mate disappears off camera with the chemist, Lo Coltello pushes Budd into her black Merc and gets into the driver's seat. As the Merc disappears off camera, Tommaso is calling Zeitgeist.

'The hunter is now the hunted,' observes Monsieur.

Zeitgeist reports that he's getting a good signal from the tracker. Seconds later, the screen flickers back into life. A large white van bowls into sight and two workmen get out. Going round to the rear of the van, they lift out a door that looks extremely heavy. They clear out the remains of the shattered door, sling the pieces in the van and fit the new door. Then they close and lock it and drive off.

With his slight smile, Tommaso comments, 'It would not do to have someone break in, would it?' He returns to the dining room to get on with his lunch.

Zeitgeist calls. 'He's out of Antibes and heading for Nice on the Corniche.'

Seconds later, the outside camera activates as a black Merc just like Gerda Budd's rolls up to the villa and parks. If I didn't know that she was a prisoner in her own car heading for Nice, this would have been quite a shock.

Becks says, 'No prizes for guessing who it

is.' And sure enough, von Schwarzberg gets out, wearing a Men in Black suit and shades. It's his balding head that gives him away. The man with him is dressed the same and has red hair and a short red beard. Becks says, 'Yuk! I hate facial hair.'

Von Schwarzberg produces a key from his pocket, unlocks the new, very heavy door and they go inside. The hall camera picks them up briefly, then they disappear. 'Gone underground,' says Becks.

Half an hour later, Zeitgeist calls again. 'They're out of Nice and heading for Monaco.' The screen stays blank. Becks opens her Law Revision Guide. For the rest of our watch, there's no more action on camera. But Zeitgeist's reports come through every time Gerda Budd's Merc reaches the next city on its journey to – where? By now, I'm starting to get an idea of where.

Monsieur comes in at three in the afternoon with coffees for us, and I update him about the dudes in the bunker. 'So, it is just as Julius and Tommaso thought. And what is Zeitgeist's latest report?'

'They're through Genova, still on the coast road, heading for La Spezia. I'll bet Lo Coltello's going to Napoli, Monsieur.'

'The HQ of the Camorra. That sounds very likely, Joe.'

Becks closes her revision guide. 'What will they do with Gerda Budd, Monsieur?'

'They will want information from her about her network. If she co-operates, she will be more use to them alive than dead.'

By the time Monsieur comes in with Dad to take over at five, Gerda Budd's Merc is well on the way to Rome. The man with the red hair and beard has gone out and come back with two bulging bags of groceries and a large takeaway pizza. 'Looks like they're definitely here for the duration,' comments Becks.

Monsieur looks at Dad. 'Now is the time to act. It will not take von Schwarzberg long to find the cameras and microphones. Once he realises that he is under observation …'

'What are you going to do, Monsieur?'

'I have briefed the Marseille Chief of Police. He is ready to send in a team of crack RAID officers.'

'Like, when Azarov set fire to the château?'

'The same – only, this time, Joe, we do not need to go with them!'

The screen suddenly flickers into life: it's the hall camera. The man with the red hair and the beard that Becks detests is looking around him, up at the ceiling and at the walls. Then, he's staring straight at us: well, at our camera. He pulls a chair across, climbs on it and his hand shoots out. It becomes huge, covering the camera and turning the screen black.

Monsieur is already on the phone to the Marseille Chief of Police.

The next morning, Monsieur and Dad update us in the Ops Room. Dad is looking more relaxed than I've seen him in a long time. 'The RAID officers rushed the bunker at 6.00 pm. They wear helmet cams and the Marseille Chief of Police thought you might like a slice of the action.'

He clicks on a link. The officer wearing the camera is running up the drive towards Gerda Budd's villa. He seems to be the one leading the charge. He must be carrying a gun because as he approaches the door, there's a bang and the lock explodes.

Now they're inside, fanning out, looking for the entrance to the bunker. There seems to be six of them. All in black and wearing body armour, like before. Then one of them shouts, 'Le voici!' He's found a door beneath the staircase that looks like a cupboard door – but it isn't. Now we're in the dark, thundering down a spiral staircase. The door into the bunker isn't locked.

What happens next is very fast. Our officer shoves the door, shouts 'Police! Ne bougez pas!' and there are von Schwarzberg and Redbeard, mouths open. Before they can reach for their guns, they've been cuffed and disarmed. Other officers are inspecting the laboratory and taking photos of all the equipment that goes into making killer drugs.

Von Schwarzberg starts to splutter something about this being outrageous. The officers nod ironically, and one says, 'Bien sûr, tu as raison, mon ami. Et maintenant c'est fini.' *How right you are, my friend. And now it's all over.*

Dad clicks off the link. 'As you can see, they caught them completely by surprise. Von Schwarzberg and Co probably assumed that the camera in the hall was part of Gerda Budd's security system – a big mistake.'

I look at Tommaso, remembering his spymaster words: *Then he will start to make mistakes. And then – we bring him down.*

Dad continues, 'Zeitgeist called to say that Lo Coltello is in Napoli – he has the co-ordinates.'

Monsieur says, 'I will share this information with the Marseille Chief of Police; what he does with it is up to him. When Lo Coltello discovers that von Schwarzberg is on his way back to prison – most probably Berlin and certainly not Dartmoor – he will have to completely reassess his own situation.'

'And that of Gerda Budd?' Becks asks.

Dad looks at Tommaso. 'Another unholy alliance, would you say, Tommaso?'

'She has too much valuable information for them to kill her. Yes, Uncle – with von Schwarzberg off the scene again, Gerda Budd and the Camorra will once more have to be unlikely allies.'

'So is our main target now Lo Coltello?'

'We do not pursue him, Uncle. We continue to feed him disinformation. The next disruption must come from a direction that he is not anticipating at all.'

Think like your enemy. You do what they are NOT expecting!

I catch Monsieur's expression as he looks at

Tommaso. This young Camorristo is teaching us all – because he's been there and got the T-shirt.

Dad says thoughtfully, 'The ship in question is due to sail from the Arctic on the 4th of August, isn't it?'

'Just under two weeks, yes Uncle …'

Just then, Monsieur's landline rings. He picks it up and answers, then switches it to speaker mode. 'It is Daha. Where are you calling from, Daha?'

'I am back in Surat, Monsieur. I heard that Tommaso has successfully hacked the Kremlin and was wondering how you are all getting on, taking the fight to the enemy?'

'I will let Tommaso tell you that, Daha.'

'Hello, Daha. So, we have sent a substantial cocaine shipment straight into the arms of the Marseille customs officials. A bunker in Antibes that was manufacturing the lethal heroin has just been busted. And the man Lo Coltello went to a great deal of trouble to release from prison is heading back inside.'

Daha laughs with delight. 'That is splendid news! And now, my friends, I have something for you. But first I am sending Monsieur a link to a news clip to give you the background. Call me when you have read it.'

Dad says, 'Let's Zoom this one. I'll set it up.'

Becks grins. 'Told you this ought to be called the Apps Room!'

The clip reads: *'THE MOST AUDACIOUS SHOPLIFT EVER'. A sophisticated gang has stolen eight million pounds worth of gems from a Monaco jewellers. Posing as reputable and wealthy Russian businessmen, they used the tactic of distraction – a phone call to the shop's gemologist from a gang member – to substitute pebbles for the real gems. The theft was not discovered until the following day, by which time the gang had returned to Russia. This is thought to be the largest value single incident of shoplifting in European criminal history. One of the nine jewels was a heart-shaped diamond which alone is reputed to be worth £2.2 million.*

Tommaso comments, 'There is really no distinction anymore between a Russian oligarch and a 'vor': Russian for *thief*.'

Sitting in his exotic apartment with its embroidered throws, and back in jeans and bare feet, Daha agrees with him. 'And now we come to the interesting part. I was approached last week by a Russian lady who introduced herself as Elena Marienska: I doubt if it was her real name. She said she had been recommended to me by a friend because of my, to quote her, 'discretion'.'

We all smile at that word. He continues, 'We met in the security of my office in Surat, and she produced a very distinctive heart-shaped diamond.' He holds up his phone to show us the video: the diamond seems to radiate beams of light.

Becks exclaims, 'The one that was stolen!'

'The same. Naturally, I simply commented on how unusual it was. So now Ms Marienska comes to the point. She wishes to know if the diamond is what she calls a 'fake'.'

'You mean, an ordinary gemstone impersonating a diamond?'

'A very good question, Becks! Her actual words were, 'Is it a real diamond? Or is it one that's been grown in a laboratory?' Which betrayed quite a degree of ignorance for a diamond thief.'

'What did you tell her?'

'I told her that it was a real diamond. And it had been grown in a laboratory.'

Tommaso comments, 'It was real because it would have exactly the same physical properties as a diamond that had been mined from the earth.'

'Precisely,' replies Daha. 'And this is where we can wage war on one of Russia's largest sources of income. Because Russia has the largest diamond mine in the world. Accounting for more than twenty five percent of global diamond production.'

Dad says, 'The Jubilee diamond mine. So if lab-grown diamonds are flooding the market, it's going to bring the price of diamonds crashing down.'

Daha nods. 'And so it should. Diamond producers deliberately keep them in short supply to inflate the price to the consumer. And yet the value of diamonds to mankind is actually beyond price.'

Monsieur says, 'The graphene windscreen layer in the Bentley is made from the same element as diamonds – crystallized pure carbon.'

Becks adds, 'My sound system uses diamond in the tweeter speakers.'

'And in the not-too-distant future,' says Dad, 'Lab-grown diamonds are going to replace the silicon chips in our computers, phones and every other gismo. Because they don't heat up like silicon and crystals, and they last – well, forever.'

'Gives a whole new meaning to the advertising, doesn't it?' replies Daha. 'The next time NASA builds a space shuttle, they'll probably use diamond for the windows.'

'Diamonds in space!' Becks exclaims.

'Diamonds have been in space for many millions of years,' replies Daha. 'The largest diamond so far found in the universe is the size of a small planet – around two thirds the size of Earth. It's a burned out star – a white dwarf.'

Becks is entranced. 'Where is this diamond planet – and what's it called?'

'It is in the constellation Centaurus, only 50 light years away. And you will love the name, Becks: the astronomers who discovered it in 2004 named it Lucy, after the song by the Beatles *Lucy in the Sky with Diamonds.*'

'The hell with becoming a lawyer – I'm going to be an astronomer!'

Daha smiles, dark eyes glowing. 'While Lucy is a dead star now, it used to shine like our Sun. So you see, diamonds are not so rare as the fat cats who profit from them would like us to believe. There was a copper age, an iron age and a steel age. Next will be diamond.'

I'm curious. 'So where does that leave you as a brillianteer, Daha?'

'I do think that a stone that has come from deep

underground and is many millions of years old has a power all its own. But the terrible wages paid to those who mine them, and the daily dangers they face, trouble me a great deal.'

'So you also have a laboratory that makes diamonds?' asks Becks. 'I mean, that stone you sent to the Indian princess in place of Monsieur's blue diamond …?'

'Ah, Becks, there is never any fooling you, is there? Yes, I have a lab.'

'So, how could you tell that the heart-shaped diamond was grown in a lab, if they're so close to the ones that come out of the ground?'

He shrugs. 'It is very hard to tell. The main reason I knew was because I myself had grown and cut that very diamond.'

'So, how did it end up in a Monaco jeweller's?'

'We are arriving at the main point of my call to you. There are two heart-shaped diamonds. The first one came out of Russia's Jubilee diamond mine and brought a fortune into the Kremlin's coffers before arriving in Monaco. The second one I grew and cut in my lab.'

'As part of your project to undermine over-inflated diamond prices?' asks Dad.

'Exactly – especially Russia's.'

'So let me guess,' says Dad. 'You managed to substitute your lab-grown diamond for the one that had come out of the ground in Russia?'

'You have it, Commander.'

'And no one at that Monaco jewellers noticed?'

'No one. Not even the thieves who then stole my lab-grown diamond.'

'And now you're going to the press to explode the news round the world with a photo of the two identical diamonds side by side – and the world diamond market will take a colossal hit!'

'I will of course return the mined diamond to the Monaco jeweller. But as he can now never be certain of its provenance, it will never again be valued at £2.2 million.'

Monsieur asks, 'And Ms Elena Marienska – how did she react when you gave your answer, Daha?'

'At first she refused to believe me. So I showed her the mined diamond that I had taken from the jewellers and replaced with the one she had stolen. She left in rather a hurry.'

Becks laughs. 'Perfect! You're a genius Daha!'

'Just doing my bit, that is all. And what is your next project, Tommaso?'

'Courtesy of the Kremlin's technological vulnerabilities, we have discovered that there will be a ship coming out of Russia via the Arctic Circle on 4th August, almost certainly carrying an illegal cargo. We are still trying to establish what that cargo is.'

'Then I will let you get back to work,' says Daha.

Becks has been busy scribbling on a piece of scrap paper. 'Before you go, Daha, I've got the headline for your diamond story!' She holds up the paper to the camera. It says *Diamonds are for everyone.*

'Would you like a job as my PR agent, Becks?'

CHAPTER 5

Hypersonic

Arriving in Monsieur's study, I find Tommaso hard at work decoding Icebreaker's translation of his latest hack into the weak computer in the Kremlin. 'I am getting closer to finding out what cargo this ship will be carrying ... Icebreaker is working on it as well.' There's a Ping! from his email. 'Ah! It is him.'

As he scans through the email, Dad comes in, followed by Monsieur. He takes one glance at the screen. 'That's the cargo? This is serious!'

'The Zircon is no ordinary cruise missile is it, Uncle?'

'It's a missile that no one has any defence against. It's hypersonic – flying at up to Mach 8. That's 9,800 kilometres per hour. And it's manoeuvrable, controlled by commands during flight – so no one knows what its target is until after it's hit.'

Tommaso brings up a Google image of a missile with wings and side rocket thrusters, about nine metres long. It makes me go cold.

'What is worse,' observes Monsieur, 'Is that the missile's high speed creates a cloud of plasma around it, absorbing radio waves and making it virtually invisible to radar.'

I'm getting colder. 'Who else has hypersonic cruise missiles?'

'China and – more recently – the US. The UK is on the case but not there yet. There was talk of developing some kind of pact between Russia, China and the US. But if Russia is making a present of these monsters to a fourth party, any pact is meaningless.'

I find I'm speaking almost in a whisper. 'Imagine what could happen if these end up in terrorist hands!'

'I'm afraid the Kremlin's aim is always to create instabilities to extend its own power,' Dad says grimly.

'What they don't realise is how easily it could backfire,' says Tommaso. 'The Kremlin has never been known for a high IQ.'

'Dad, can't we get the Navy onto it?'

'If the Navy grabs a Russian ship that turns out not to have cruise missiles on board, it would create a diplomatic crisis of mammoth proportions. It could even trigger hostilities.'

'Right – but if we were absolutely certain that this Russian ship DOES have Zircon missiles, could they intervene then?'

'Difficult to see how. They can't fire on it. And, if it's a remote controlled vessel like the Alyona, they can't force it into a British port.'

Tommaso says, 'So Joe and I get on board this remote-controlled ship while it is en route. We verify what it is carrying. If it is illegal arms, I hack its onboard computer to take control. Then, escorted by the Navy, we follow a course that will take the ship to a destination of their choice.'

'How would you get on board?'

I know the answer to this one. 'The ship will very likely be taking a route similar to the Alyona, past the North West coast of Scotland. If the weather's too rough for us to use Monsieur's copter and get winched onto the deck, we ask Isla to take us out to the ship in Sea Eagle. I know she'd be up for it when we explain why!'

'So, you'd climb up the rope ladder that the pilot normally uses?'

'Something like that.'

Monsieur looks at Dad. 'I believe these young commandos can do this.'

Dad agrees. 'But there's a lot of intelligence we still need to get hold of. Firstly, what ship are we talking about? Second, is it remote-controlled? And third, how much can we find out about its actual course?'

Tommaso is clicking on an email. 'We have the answer to the first question, Uncle. Icebreaker tells me the ship is called Arctic Ocean. He has sent some specification details.'

—m—

While Tommaso and Icebreaker are trying to establish whether the Arctic Ocean is remote-controlled, I trawl through the specification to get an idea of what boarding it is going to be like. Becks joins me with coffees.

'She's bigger than the Alyona was; length is 177 metres. So there's going to be quite a height to climb up that rope ladder.'

She points out, 'Althought it'll be less of a climb if she's fully loaded, because she'll be lower in the water.'

'True. And if it's a bit rough, a fully loaded ship will be moving around less than a lighter one.'

'Until the cargo comes loose.'

'Don't let's go there Becks!' The memory of that perfect storm of nuclear reactor in meltdown, lunatic Russian remote-controlling the ship, locked on course for the third largest whirlpool in the world and then the cargo coming loose will remain with us forever. 'I think it's time I called Isla.'

She picks up straightaway. 'Joe, that is so weird. I was just about to call you! You OK?'

'We're good, Isla. What were you going to call about?'

'The fishing fleets off the North West coast have all received a warning about some Russian ships trying to create their own shipping lanes. Instead of sticking to the Irish Sea, they're dodging and weaving between the Outer Hebrides and Skye, where most of the fishing fleets operate.'

'Result, chaos?'

'There's been collisions in fog, where our boys have come off worse. These are big cargo ships.'

'Around 600 feet long?'

'Exactly so. Quite a lot bigger than the Alyona.'

'I was just discussing that with Becks. And I have a huge favour to ask you, Isla … It's a really big ask.'

I give her the full story about the Arctic Ocean and what she'll be carrying on the 4th August.

'Dear God, Joe. This could start World War Three! How can I help?'

'If she's remote-controlled, Tommaso and I are aiming to board her. He'll hack the onboard computer to take control. Then the plan is we have an escort from the Navy to a destination of their choosing.'

'You want me to take you out to the ship?'

'It's a big call Isla, but – yes, please.'

'Happy to oblige. We'll use Sea Eagle; it'll give us maximum stability when you're getting onto the pilot's ladder. Can you send me as much spec as you've got on Arctic Ocean?'

'That is so brilliant Isla! There's just no way we can do this without you!'

'These Ruskies are disrupting our fishing, Joe. If we can disrupt THEM, count me in!'

Dad looks round in surprise as I charge into the Ops Room. 'I've just spoken to Isla. She's right up for it. And she gave me some great info about the Arctic Ocean's likely course. She said the fishing fleets have been warned to steer clear of Russian ships that are following a Southwards course between the Outer Hebrides and the Isle of Skye, instead of sticking to the Irish Sea.'

He brings up a map of the Highlands and Islands. 'This is shaping up nicely. Now we just need the make or break info – is she remote-controlled?'

'Because if she's not, we need a Plan B.'

Dad says, 'I'm not sure if there is a Plan B.'

At that moment, Tommaso comes in. His face is inscrutable. 'I have some news.' He pauses and I think, well that's it. Then he smiles his slight smile. 'The Arctic Ocean is remote-controlled.'

'Right,' says Dad, 'Let training begin: ship-to-ship boarding in foul weather.'

'I just need to send the ship's spec to Isla, Dad.'

While I'm sending her the spec from my phone, Dad brings up a YouTube clip about the incredibly brave seamen who pilot ships safely into harbour from the high seas. 'I want you to watch this clip of a pilot boarding the ship he's going to navigate into harbour. It's blowing a Force nine. The ship and the pilot boat are pitching and rolling all over the place. Wave height is around ten feet. This pilot is doing a perfect transfer. I want you to tell me all the things that could possibly go wrong.' He clicks on Play.

We're watching the scene from a camera on the pilot boat, and I can almost feel the up and down movement as she's tossed about on the waves. The ship towers above the little boat, rolling from side to side in slow motion.

And I begin to see what could go wrong. From

the pilot boat being on top of a wave to being in the trough of a wave, there's a huge difference in height in relation to the rope ladder that's fixed to the side of the ship. As we get closer to the ship, it rolls towards us. There's only our fenders between us and this monster, which looks like it could so easily push us under the sea. How the captain of the pilot boat manages to avoid being crushed by the ship is beyond me.

Then I spot another potential disaster. If the ship is rolling towards the pilot boat when the pilot steps onto the ladder, it's going to be impossible to climb the ladder. And so easy to fall into the sea. Where he'll be crushed between the ship and the boat.

Holding my breath, I watch as the pilot boat slides alongside the huge ship, and moves with it in the surging waves. The pilot is standing ready, watching the roll of the ship and the height of the waves. Now the pilot boat is at the top of a wave and the ship is just starting to roll away from him. He steps smoothly onto the ladder, grasping it firmly. And the roll of the ship makes his climb less vertical. He's more on top of things rather than upside down. But he climbs very fast, before the ship starts to roll the other way.

'So,' says Dad, 'What went right?'

'He waited until they were at the top of a wave and the ship was starting to roll away from the pilot boat?'

'Absolutely essential if you want to stay alive. What else could go wrong?'

Tommaso says, 'In rough seas like this, the ship could hit the pilot boat. There is also the possibility that the pilot boat could become hung up on the ship's side.'

'Correct. And what problems could you have once you've boarded?'

'The deck could be running with sea water. And there may be few handholds to avoid getting thrown into the sea.'

Dad nods. 'You've no lifeline supporting you when you're on that ladder, and nothing to clip yourself onto when you're on deck. You can't take any of the precautions that you normally would.'

I look at Tommaso. 'You've done this before, haven't you?'

He smiles that slight smile. 'The Camorra are not averse to a spot of piracy, Joe. There are very few crew on supertankers. They are at their most vulnerable when queuing to go into port.'

Dad shuts down the clip, saying casually to Tommaso, 'So, now that Dieter is on his way back behind bars, and in Berlin where he'll remain, that sets me free?'

'Just because von Schwarzberg is in prison for life doesn't mean that Lo Coltello has lost interest in you, Uncle. He still has you on radar lock.'

Dad replies, like he's half-joking, 'So now it's time for me to bring *him* in!'

I hope he is joking.

Now we know what we're intercepting and where, preparations go right ahead. Monsieur decides that we'll need both the copter and the Bentley. So he and Tommaso set about pre-flight checks while I give the Bentley a once-over in the old barn where it's housed.

Feels weird doing this without Becks, but I'm so happy that she's decided to pass on this project and concentrate on her exams. Tommaso and I have got exams too, before we set off for North West Scotland, but they're not as important as hers. After Becks and I appeared as witnesses in the trial where justice was finally done to Monsieur's tragic past, she's totally focused on becoming a barrister. She'll be brilliant.

She comes in at six to tell me supper's going to be served in half an hour; then stays to help me finish the checks. 'D'you want to take an extra underwater tracker, just in case?'

'Came in handy last time, didn't it?'

She takes the tracker from one of the large wooden chests that line the stone walls of the barn. 'Have you checked the Raptor?'

'Monsieur's been deploying it regularly around the grounds while our German friend was a threat. It's good.'

She tucks the tracker into the Bentley boot with the Velociraptor. 'I guess with von Schwarzberg back in his box, we can all relax a teeny bit?'

'I don't think Dad can, with Lo Coltello still on the loose.'

'Trouble is, he doesn't seem to think so, does he?'

'He doesn't understand the Camorra mindset like Tommaso does.'

'So he's dying to get back out there to track down The Knife ...'

'Which is just what they want. And they're prepared to wait it out until he runs out of patience, being stuck here.'

'You're really worried about your Dad, aren't you Joe?'

'Not just worried, Becks. I'm scared.'

'Has there been any more news from Zeitgeist about the tracker he fitted to the Merc?'

'It's been quiet for a while: he reckons they've found it. So Lo Coltello could be anywhere now. C'mon, let's go eat, I'm starving.'

She picks up the remote and locks the Bentley, saying, 'Joe, is it OK, me not coming on this one? I sort of feel that I'm letting you down?'

Gently I take the remote from her and wrap her in my arms. 'It's very OK, Becks. Just ace those exams and give me your autograph when you're a famous barrister.'

Unlike my previous experiences at school in England, the exams go smoothly and I put them behind me. And now, all I can think about is that ship, the Arctic Ocean, and its lethal cargo. We're setting off tomorrow for the North West coast of Scotland – me driving the Bentley and Tommaso co-piloting Monsieur in the copter.

Over supper, Monsieur updates us on his discussions with the Navy. 'They have put me in direct contact with the commander of the Edinburgh.'

'The frigate that rescued us from Azarov's copter – fantastic!'

'It helps greatly that we have worked together before. They agree that the Navy cannot be involved in the interception of a Russian ship. However, as soon as there is proof that the cargo of the Arctic Ocean is missiles – hypersonic or subsonic, it doesn't matter – they will move in.'

'So if Tommaso and I send you a photo, you can forward it to the Edinburgh?'

'Make it many photos and include yourselves.'

Dad comes in. 'Just heard from Icebreaker. The Arctic Ocean sailed from the port of Murmansk at four thirty this afternoon.'

At 5.00 a.m. the following morning, the roaring rotors flatten the long grass in the paddock as Monsieur and Tommaso lift off. Surrounded by the wood and leather of the Bentley, I ease through on a light throttle as the wrought iron gates swing open, and close behind me.

And just as I check in my rear view mirror to

make sure that the gates are closed, I see a shadowy figure flit across my field of vision. So quickly, I might even have imagined it. But I haven't imagined it. Someone is watching the gates to the château.

On that long road towards Kyle of Lochalsh on the North West coast of Scotland, I ask myself the impossible question. I can't tell Dad. That would be the surest possible way of getting him out of those gates trying to hunt down the culprit. Except that the Camorra will get to him first. I can't tell Tommaso or Monsieur – they're busy flying a helicopter to try and stop World War Three.

In the end, on the ferry from Calais to Dover, Precious safely stowed alongside more humble vehicles on the car decks, I phone a friend. My best friend.

'I'll tell him, Joe. I'll make him take it seriously. I'll also contact the Marseille police.'

'Thanks, Becks. Only you can do this.'

'Your dad can be very pig-headed, Joe. I now know where you get it from.'

'He is scaring the hell out of me, Becks.'

'I know. I'll do my absolute best – now, take care with that ship-to-ship stuff.'

'And have a great law exam tomorrow.'

'Thanks – I can't wait to get my teeth into it!'

After the call to Becks, I go down onto the car decks. Not to check up on the Bentley: it's well-protected against anyone who might try to interfere with it. I'm down here to check up on a car that's been following me for hundreds of miles.

It might have been following ever since I left the château, but I was too preoccupied with the stalker to notice. I lost sight of it queuing to get on the ferry. And the problem is, it was at too great a distance for me to see the number plate. Also, there could be a great many black Merc coupes on this boat. So I won't know for sure until after I come off at Dover.

My mobile goes as I arrive at black Merc coupe number two. It's Becks. 'I'm not sure how seriously your dad's taking this, but the police certainly are – they're sending a car to take me in to my exam tomorrow.'

'Glad to hear it. What time does your exam finish?'

'Three thirty. The police are taking me home too.'

'Good. I'll call you after three thirty tomorrow. Now take care.'

'You too!'

I have no intention of telling Becks about the Merc. She's got enough on her plate. At this point I've had it with tracking down Mercs, so I wander into the restaurant for a burger and coffee, and an hour's sleep in a chair.

When I wake up, the white cliffs of Dover are on the horizon. Soon, I'll be driving through the night to Scotland. And so of course, I'll have no idea whether the headlamps in my rear view mirror belong to a black Merc coupe or a white van.

It's dark by the time I've got London well behind me. At Bracknell services I pull over for another snooze followed by a Starbucks. As I come back to the car with the coffee in hand, I pass a black Merc coupe with heavily tinted windows. There's no driver. So perhaps he or she was standing behind me in the queue in Starbucks.

I glance over my shoulder. There's no one behind me but that doesn't mean a thing. I gulp down the rest of the coffee, bin the cup and jump into the Bentley. Whoever it might be is about to get a run for their money.

After a high-speed sprint, I slow down at Swindon. You don't take any chances here: Swindon is the home of Very Efficient Cops. I can't see any sign of a black Merc coupe behind me. But then a thought strikes me, quite a bit later than it should have done.

I pull into Membury services and conduct a thorough examination of the Bentley's wheelarches. Must look quite funny, this dude lying on his back in the car park, shining a torch at the underside of a very beautiful, very expensive car.

And tucked into the nearside rear wheelarch, there it is. They must have fitted the tracker while I was in Starbucks. Then I think, No: the golden opportunity was on the ferry. I've been making it so easy for them. I nearly grind the thing beneath my heel, then think better of it. They can conclude that I've decided to spend the night at Membury services. I chuck it into a rubbish bin and hit the road.

By half four, I'm nearing Glasgow: time to call Becks.

'It was tough, but I'm – how do they put it? – quietly confident.'

'I bet you smashed it.'

'The police car's just pulling into the college carpark. Everyone'll think I'm being arrested. Where are you?'

'Glasgow, thanks to a weirdly uncongested M6. Now in you get and stay safe.'

—⚬—

It's getting dark as I approach the cottage that Monsieur has rented for this mission to the Highlands. The cottage has a paddock for Monsieur's copter to land in, and I can see the rotors at rest, dimly in the twilight. As I get out of the Bentley, inhaing the scent of pine trees, the front door opens and Tommaso comes out. A wonderful smell of beef stew follows him. I suddenly realise that I'm ravenous.

We hug like reunited brothers. 'Monsieur is cooking boeuf en daube. How was your journey, Joe?'

'Interesting.' We get the wetsuits and my overnight bag out of the car and go inside. Monsieur is putting loaded plates on the table. 'Perfect timing, Joe.'

Over supper I tell them about the stalker at the gates, Becks' new chauffeurs and my follower.

Tommaso looks unsurprised. 'I'm afraid it is standard Camorra practice.'

'I am very glad the police took it seriously,' Monsieur comments.

'I wish Dad would, Monsieur.'

'You are worried that he may be tempted to go after Lo Coltello? So are we all, Joe.'

―⁓―

It's a six o'clock start the next morning in the copter: we're going on a reconnoitring trip. With Tommaso co-piloting and me in in the back seat, we lift off from the paddock into clear dawn skies.

On the way to Kyle of Lochalsh, Monsieur updates Tommaso and me on his latest communication with the Edinburgh. 'Commander Airdrie tells me they are currently positioned just North of Shetland, which is Scotland's northernmost island. He is expecting to see the Arctic Ocean on their radar shortly after midday today. Thereafter they will be shadowing it and keeping us informed.'

'And we're going to overfly the stretch of water where these other Russian ships keep crashing into fishing trawlers?'

'Because it's very likely the route that the Arctic Ocean will take, yes Joe. That is, as Isla said, between the Isle of Skye and the Outer Hebrides."

'I bet all these Russian ships are remote controlled and that's why they keep bumping into other boats.'

Tommaso gives his slight smile, 'You are probably right, Joe. Do we know roughly what time tomorrow the Arctic Ocean will be in that area, Monsieur?'

'Commander Airdrie says she will enter that part of the sea called the Minch at around eight in the morning. He will have a more precise timing once she's on the Edinburgh's radar.'

I look down. Below us are the Isle of Skye and opposite across a narrow stretch of water the township of Kyle of Lochalsh with its harbour and rail station. Where the two headlands are closest, the beautiful white Skye bridge joins them in a flying arch.

I remember the huge Lion's Mane jellyfish floating in the harbour when we first came to Kyle in my desperate search for Dad. And it's horrible that I feel just as worried about him now as I did then.

Now we're flying over the Isle of Skye, with its craggy backbone that makes it such a white knuckle mountain bike ride. Beyond Skye, faint as a dream on the horizon, is the outline of the Outer Hebridean islands. A fishing trawler looks like a toy on the blue green sea. So this is the vast amphitheatre where our Arctic Ocean drama will play out tomorrow.

I look down at the restless waves far below. 'Do we know the forecast for tomorrow, Monsieur?'

He's pulling the copter gently round in a large arc, turning back towards Kyle of Lochalsh. 'Not good, I'm afraid, Joe.'

Tommaso checks on his phone. 'It is unchanged. Gale Force six, gusting seven; rising to Storm Force ten, maybe eleven.'

'Right.' The last time I heard a forecast like that, Becks and I were on Monsieur's yacht, and he was being forced to sail straight into the teeth of the Storm From Hell.

Tommaso says, 'We have to get on board before the wind gets to Storm Force.'

'Isla agrees that we need to catch the ship as far North as possible. Preferably as she enters that part of the sea between Skye and the Outer Hebrides called the Minch.'

'That's around eight in the morning isn't it Monsieur?'

He straightens out the copter and we start to fly back over Skye. 'Isla says we need to allow two hours at least if we are to intercept the ship at that point. Which means leaving harbour at five in the morning.'

On the way back over Skye, an officer on the Edinburgh calls Monsieur's mobile and Tommaso takes it. He passes on the message to me and Monsieur. 'They now have the Arctic Ocean on their radar. So they can now give a more precise time when the ship enters the Minch, where we need to board her. He reckons it at 8.10 a.m., if she continues at her present speed.'

'Good.' Monsieur puts the copter into a gradual descent as we fly over Kyle of Lochalsh and the white Skye Bridge. 'Can you pass his message on to

Isla, please Tommaso. And then find us the nearest refuelling point.'

Once back at the cottage, Monsieur serves up the remains of the beef stew and then tells me and Tommaso to get some sleep. 'The way current timings are, we will be leaving here for Kyle at 4.00 a.m. – but if the Arctic Ocean increases her speed, those timings will change.'

'Suppose I get the wetsuits and other gear loaded into the Bentley now, Monsieur?'

'A good plan, Joe.'

When I get back into the cottage Monsieur is on his mobile, talking to the Edinburgh. He's going to be on watch all night, in case things change.

Before I turn in, I call Becks. 'The Marseille police are being amazing, Joe. They're driving me in to all my exams and bringing me home. My mates never stop ragging me that as soon as I'm done with the exams I'll be in court – but in the dock!'

'Are they keeping an eye on the gates?'

'They're doing regular patrols. Which means that Grandad, Mum and Madame de L'Ētang can now go for walks in the grounds. And all the groceries are being delivered.'

'And Talia and Arnaud – still on their History of Art course in Seville?'

'They're doing a summer extension, they're loving it so much.'

'I bet Jack's got no plans to come back yet from Juilliard either?'

'We Zoomed this evening; his band is getting all these gigs.'

'And Dad? Still restless?'

'He can't ignore the police car and the patrols …'

'But he doesn't want to be there. Maybe he should have been part of this mission.'

'You know you don't mean that, Joe. Until Lo Coltello's dealt with, I'm afraid your Dad is a marked man.'

'I wish he could understand that, Becks. You got many more exams?'

'Last one's tomorrow. Maths. Bring it on! How is it with you?'

'Monsieur is a classy chef. We had boeuf en daube.'

'You're making my mouth water! Everything else lining up OK?'

'It's all good. Have a great Maths exam.' I don't mention the weather forecast.

―⁂―

At half four the following morning, dawn is just showing very dimly over the mountains of the Highlands. Monsieur is driving, Tommaso is in front on his laptop and I'm still trying to get my eyes open. Tommaso closes the laptop. 'The signal is poor – should be better once we get to the harbour.'

'So, as soon as we're aboard Sea Eagle, you're going to start hacking the Arctic Ocean?'

'I need to be in control before we board her. First, I need to reduce her speed to make it easy as possible for us to get up that rope ladder. The officer who called us yesterday from the Edinburgh said she was doing twenty knots. I need to slow her to six or seven.'

'Because we still need her moving rather than stationary, as she'll be more stable?'

He nods. 'And so will Sea Eagle.'

The sky is slowly lightening, pale sun gleaming on Sea Eagle's white hull, as the Bentley parks on the quayside. Clad in her usual white oilies, with her tousled blonde hair, Isla greets us warmly. 'One of these days we'll all get together over a meal when there's not some kind of massive emergency going on! Right, let's get you settled on board.'

As we go up the gangplank, I cast a quick glance at the waves. They're choppy, and playful gusts are buffeting my face. By the time we're out to sea, this could very easily turn into a Gale Force six gusting seven. We don't want to be trying to board the Arctic Ocean in anything much stronger than that.

In the control cabin, Isla finds a space for Tommaso's laptop, and he gets to work. She starts the engine and the mighty marine diesel rumbles into life. The anchor rattles up into its housing and one of the crew members on shore chucks the mooring line to Monsieur. Then we're drifting slowly backwards off the mooring and turning towards the North West.

'Commander Airdrie was in touch just before you arrived.' Isla twitches the wheel slightly to correct her course. 'He says the Arctic Ocean is still doing twenty knots and due to arrive at the Minch at 8.10 a.m. – so I guess you'd be aiming to get that speed down, Tommaso?'

'If I bring it down to six or seven?'

'That'll do nicely. Now, I don't like the forecast any more than you guys, so I'll be putting on all speed to get us to that ship as quickly as possible.'

'Did Commander Airdrie comment on the conditions that they're experiencing off Shetland?'

'Gale Force seven, rising, Joe. But there's nearly always a gale blowing that far North.'

Monsieur comes into the cabin and passes round flasks of coffee – 'And one for the Captain. This would not be possible without you, Isla.'

'These Ruskies are being a dratted nuisance, Christian. And if Arctic Ocean's carrying what you think she is, then doing nothing is not an option.'

Tommaso looks up from his laptop. 'Has Commander Airdrie said what destination he wants us to take her to, if she is carrying Zircons?'

Isla shakes her head. 'For security, he won't mention anything in radio comms, Tommaso. He'll more likely send you encrypted co-ordinates to program into the autopilot.'

I look out of the cabin window. Rain is starting to lash the glass, and the waves have foaming crests. Sea Eagle must be doing at least twenty knots; the Isle of Skye on our port side is fast receding.

An hour later, there's a brief message from the Edinburgh. The Arctic Ocean is still on time for the Minch. They send Isla the ship's trajectory so that she can set Sea Eagle on course for the intercept. The dawn is now darkened by a sky wracked with torn black clouds, and the wind has become a low howl. Isla says, 'At the speed we've been doing, we'll meet up with her before she reaches the Minch – and hopefully before things get too much rougher.'

Tommaso says, 'I've hacked her satellite communication system. I'm now going into her ECDIS – the electronic chart display system she uses to navigate.'

'That's brilliant, bro!'

He smiles his thin smile. 'It was not too difficult. The ship is using a really ancient operating system – Windows NT.'

Half an hour later, he tells us, 'I can now control the ship's speed. Taking it down to six knots.'

Isla says, 'I've just picked her up on the radar. She's only two nautical miles away now.'

Monsieur gets on his phone, 'I will let the Edinburgh know.'

Another ten minutes, and Tommaso says, 'And

now I have the rudder. Time to put on the wetsuits, Joe.'

We go below to get changed. When we arrive back in the control cabin, wet-suited and booted, Monsieur hands us lifejackets. 'They are fitted with flares.'

Just at that moment, Isla exclaims, 'There she is!' She passes her binoculars to Tommaso. On the horizon is a ship that looks like a much larger version of the Alyona. 'I'll get us into position to run alongside her.' Isla takes back the wheel from Monsieur and cuts Sea Eagle's speed.

Sighting through the binoculars I can see the ship in close-up. She has a tall control tower and two large cranes amidships. Her bow is shaped like an icebreaker; a ship fully capable of cutting her way through the Arctic. A large proportion of the cargo, whatever it is, has been stowed on deck and covered with tarpaulins.

She looks so like the Alyona, only a lot bigger, that it makes me shiver slightly. About two hundred nautical miles south from where we are now, the Alyona lies at the bottom of the sea. Monsieur said that, with the presence of the whirlpool and the depth of the ocean, no one will ever be able to salvage her cargo. And we never did find out what that cargo was. Now, we absolutely have to discover what the Arctic Ocean is carrying.

The waves are bigger than they were when we set out and rain is still battering the windows of the control room. But this doesn't look like Storm

Force – not yet, anyway. Isla is steering Sea Eagle in a wide arc to turn and run alongside the Arctic Ocean. The ship is travelling more slowly now, thanks to Tommaso's skilful hacking.

Monsieur is talking to Commander Airdrie on the Edinburgh. He turns to us. 'He says they have both vessels on their radar now. He warns us that the wind force is rising rapidly, so to proceed with the ship-to-ship transfer as soon as possible.'

The Arctic Ocean is now around two hundred metres away, and Sea Eagle is completing a 180 degree turn that will set her on the same course as the ship. Slowly, with perfect accuracy, Isla steers Sea Eagle past the ship's stern and eases alongside her. Now I can see the rope ladder attached to the ship's side.

And it's all just like the video – this huge ship is towering above us and continually wallowing towards us then rolling away. The difference in height from the rope ladder when Sea Eagle is in the trough of a wave must be easily three metres. We cannot afford to get this wrong. Tommaso closes his laptop, zips it into its waterproof bag and slings it over his shoulders.

Now we're right alongside the ladder. 'On deck, Monsieur?'

He nods. 'Remember your training Joe!'

Out on deck, the wind hits us with mighty blasts. Tommaso says, 'I will go first – watch my timing and do the same, Joe. You will be fine.'

Now we're in the trough and the ship is rolling

towards us. The ladder is as far away from us as it's going to get. Now we're rising out of the trough and the ladder is perfectly positioned, as the ship starts to roll away from us. At that exact moment, Tommaso steps onto the ladder, grasps the side ropes and pulls himself quickly up the side of the ship: a ship where the side is far taller than your average house. At the top, he vaults over the side and waves down to me, shouting above the roar of the wind, 'I will tell you when!' And the process repeats itself, with wave trough, ship rolling towards me, ladder far away; then out of trough, ladder approaching, ship just starting to roll away. 'NOW Joe!'

And for once, one of my life's more terrifying events goes like clockwork. I step onto the ladder, climb this mountain to the top as quickly as I can and get onto the deck just as the ship is starting to roll back towards Sea Eagle. In the cabin, Isla gives us a thumbs up, then steers away to safety. Tommaso and I slap a high five.

Then we start to look for the cargo.

CHAPTER 6

Stairway To Hell

The wind is rising to a banshee howl as we slip and slide our way along the deck to the tarpaulin-lashed cargo. The ship, all 580 feet of her, is starting to pitch and roll more steeply as we hit waves that are nearing fifteen feet. The sky is now black with ragged clouds that are bombarding us with icy needles of rain. I feel incredibly grateful to Isla for getting us here ahead of the storm. I would have struggled to board the Arctic Ocean in this.

Tommaso whips his knife from his lifejacket and slices into the ropes tying the tarpaulins to whatever is beneath. We rip the tarps off. Exposing the wood of large pine trees, strapped one on top of the other.

'We need to do a representative check – so six more!' Six more slipping and sliding journeys, six more slashing attacks on the tarps – and six more piles of lashed pine trees. Tommaso is unsurprised. 'This is what they will usually do to conceal the real cargo. So now, we go below decks.'

Fighting our way back to the control tower, we find the steps that take us down to the first hold. 'How many below decks are there, Tommaso?'

'That is what they don't want anyone to know, Joe.'

It's completely dark down here, so we both use our phone torches. The ship is still moving around so much that we have to grab hold of anything we can. And there are weird, hollow clanking noises beneath us that make me wonder what kind of shape this ship is in. The memory of the Alyona hits me and I push it behind me.

Tommaso's heading over towards another pile of huge long shapes wrapped in tarps. His keen knife slashes at the ropes and we yank the tarps away. More pine trees. Tommaso says, 'Again, six more investigations. Do not be discouraged, Joe. If there are cruise missiles on this ship, there will only be two or three.'

Six investigations later, with more pine trees, I look at Tommaso: 'Well, that's it, isn't it? No cruise missiles.'

His voice is thoughtful. 'Do you remember from the spec that Icebreaker sent, how much depth below the waterline this ship has when it is fully loaded, Joe?'

'About ten metres, wasn't it?'

'So, would you say that there could be another deck below this one?'

'I guess I would. But the steps stopped on this deck.'

'So there must be a hidden access to the very lowest deck.'

The storm above us is reaching new heights

of violence. The deck we're trying to stand on is throwing us around, and the groaning and clanking sound effects below us are deafening. But Tommaso knows exactly what he's doing. Crouching at the base of where the steps seem to end, he feels around. Levers his knife into a crack. And lifts up boards, one by one, to reveal steps that continue down onto the deck that no one wants us to know about.

Torches pointing beams of light, hanging on like limpets, we descend this final stairway into Hell. Below us we can see three long, dark shapes that dimly reflect the light from our torches. They're around nine metres long, like the images Tommaso conjured from the internet. Staggering with every lurch of the ship, we make our way to the front ends of these monsters. And there are the side rocket thrusters that steer them. 'They're Zircons, aren't they?'

'Joe, while I shine the torch, can you take photos? Take a great many. And also we need selfies of ourselves next to the missiles, to prove that we haven't faked the shots.'

I click shot after shot of the long, lethal shapes. The show above us is rising in intensity. And, as we both pose unsmilingly for the most unusual selfies ever, I realise that the clanking is these beasts actually banging together. The Russians haven't bothered to gift wrap them. They've just dumped them in the hold. Tommaso says, 'We'll have to send the photos from the control room. There is no signal down here.'

As we clamber back up to the top deck, it's clear that the Arctic Ocean isn't handling a Storm Force ten going on eleven very well. The ship is pitching and rolling so much that we're almost thrown over the side as we fight our way back to the control tower.

We rush up the steps to the control room, stopping to peer inside cautiously, just in case someone's there. But there's just an array of screens and gauges similar to the Alyona. Including, happy memories, the display showing the temperature and pressure of the nuclear reactor powering the ship. Then I look out to sea, and the sight of Isla's white trawler on our starboard side is immensely reassuring.

Tommaso gets out his laptop and copies the photos from my phone. 'It is always a good plan to have a backup.'

His phone buzzes; I take it. Monsieur's voice has a shade of tension.'How goes it?'

'We've found the Zircons, Monsieur. Tommaso is sending the photos to you now.'

'I will forward them to Commander Airdrie. Now, there is a change of plan. The Edinburgh has identified a Russian destroyer following the same course as the Arctic Ocean. It is highly likely that they are aware the Ocean has been hacked, from its change of speed.'

'How far away are they?'

'Not close enough to have you on their radar, yet. Commander Airdrie says that when the

Russian ship comes within 200 kilometres of the Edinburgh, he will be able to jam their radar. But in the meantime, you need to take evasive action.'

'What does Commander Airdrie want us to do, Monsieur?'

'The destroyer will assume that you are heading for Faslane on the river Clyde, the Navy's Scottish HQ.'

'So, we do what they are not expecting, Monsieur?'

'Exactly, Joe. You must change course, for Scapa Flow in the Orkney Islands. It involves going North instead of South towards Faslane.'

'Right.'

'We will be escorting you in Sea Eagle, while the Edinburgh shadows the destroyer. I will be back in touch as soon as I have sent the photos.'

On his laptop, Tommaso is sending a command to the Arctic Ocean's navigation system. 'We are re-routing.' Slowly, pitching and rolling in waves that are now topping twenty feet, the ship is turning. 'When Monsieur calls back, can you ask him for the course setting that will steer us through all the World War wrecks in Scapa Flow? The locations of the wrecks are well publicised and I am sure that Isla will have them.'

'So it's like, a fighting ships' graveyard?'

His voice is quiet and respectful. 'It is a historical

monument, Joe, as well as one of the largest natural harbours in the world. So many ships from World Wars One and Two lie there. But the depth is sometimes only thirty metres. With the draught of this ship, we need to be very careful.'

I stare out of the control room window at the black bellies of the clouds and the mountainous, steel grey waves. 'It's pretty ironic, isn't it, that a ship whose cargo could detonate a third world war should seek shelter in Scapa Flow.'

—ᴡ—

Monsieur calls back a few minutes later. 'Commander Airdrie sends his congratulations to you both. The Navy now has abundant evidence for ensuring that the Arctic Ocean never reaches her destination.'

'Did he say where he thought she could be going, Monsieur?'

'He did not speculate. But if Tommaso could share all the hacked data that led to this intercept, he would be grateful. Now, Isla has sent the data about the wreck locations to Tommaso. Sea Eagle will take up position ahead of you and we will proceed at full power towards Scapa Flow.'

'I have the data,' says Tommaso. He's set up his laptop beside a large screen at the side of the control room, where there are two seats on pedestals secured to the floor. Relieved not to be continually sliding around and hanging on, we sit down. He taps in a few commands, and the screen displays our course. 'Here we are, just leaving the Minch. We are keeping to Westwards and rounding Cape Wrath at a good distance.'

'Because the Russian destroyer will be heading that way, going South?'

He nods. 'The Edinburgh will already have begun to mislead the destroyer's radar. As soon as she passes Shetland, where the Edinburgh is lying in wait, the Royal Navy frigate will start to shadow the destroyer.'

'So we'll be like ships passing in the night – it might as well be night, it's so dark.'

'The destroyer going South, thinking it's on our tail. And us going North to a place of safety.'

'You said the Edinburgh's radar system can mislead the Russian radar – how does that compare with jamming it?'

Tommaso smiles his thin smile. 'With radar jamming, you're aware that it's happening. A lot of noise is created and you know that the enemy is having a go at you. With the Navy's state-of-the-art system, it can fool the Russian into thinking that its radar is working normally, while sending misleading signals about location.'

'Blimey, that's clever.'

'It's even more clever than that, Joe. For a start, the Navy's system fitted to its frigates cannot be jammed. And it's so efficient that it can identify a target the size of a tennis ball travelling at Mach 3 – that's 2000 mph – at a distance greater than 25 kilometres away.'

'Sounds like it's going to be a bit of an uneven battle for the Russian.'

'Commander Airdrie has identified her as the Admiral Chabanenko. It's the same as the computers in the Kremlin, Joe. Out of date and therefore very vulnerable.'

We hang on to our chairs as a particularly vicious wave smashes into the control room window and the ship pitches at a sharp angle. There's a muffled clunking from the lowest deck. I look to starboard. 'There goes Sea Eagle.' The white trawler overtakes us, then pulls in front of our prow. At first, we can't see her at all because of the height of the ship we're on. Then, we see her pulling ahead.

'She is doing twenty knots,' says Tommaso. 'And we know that this ship can do that. I will leave half a mile distance between us.'

'How far is it to Scapa Flow?'

Tommaso brings up an overhead view on his laptop. 'Around two hundred miles from where we are now. You see how the Orkney islands form this huge natural harbour, Joe?'

For some time, my stomach's been rumbling. Things are now getting critical. 'Before we admire the harbour, can I just look for some food?' On the Alyona, Becks and I found a heaven-sent store of Mars bars in one of the control room cupboards. This time, I rummage in vain. 'I wonder if Isla's got anything they could send us by drone from Sea Eagle?'

'They are going to be far too busy to think about

food, Joe. The storm is slowly subsiding and the forecast is for clear skies tonight. You know what that means.'

'More Russian lunatics in helicopter gunships?'

'Very likely. When they find out that their destroyer has been seen off by the Navy, they will try any means of preventing their ship from falling into the wrong hands.'

'Even if that means blowing it up?'

'Russia cannot be seen to be sending hypersonic cruise missiles to foreign powers or terrorist groups. They don't mind breaking international law, which they do all the time. But they don't want to be caught.'

'So we could end up being scuttled in Scapa Flow, just like all those World War wrecks.'

'I'm sure that the Navy is aware of the risk. If another frigate can take over the shadowing of the Russian destroyer, then the Edinburgh can come to our defence.'

As he's saying that, his mobile goes. It's Monsieur, and I can tell that he and Tommaso are discussing exactly what we just have. I glance out of the control room window at the sky. It's rapidly getting dark but the storm clouds are retreating. The wave level is more ten feet than fifteen to twenty; and the wind isn't bashing the glass so relentlessly. So we could well have more visitors, this time airborne. What it is to be popular.

Tommaso says, 'Commander Airdrie has been in touch. It is pretty much as we discussed, Joe. He has handed the shadowing of the Admiral Chabanenko to two frigates that have been deployed from the Navy's Faslane HQ. He is now making all speed towards us.'

'Did he give any idea when he might catch up?'

'An hour and a half. Possibly sooner. Their frigates are very fast.'

'And very well armed.' I remember how effectively the Edinburgh frightened off Azarov's monstrous helicopter gunship when it was just about to fire on us, that time when we were following the Theseus towards the stealth ship. The single shot they fired detonated so close to the Russian copter that it must have nearly blown it out of the sky without even hitting it.

'So where do you reckon we'll be in an hour and a half?'

He brings up the navigation display. 'At the speed we're doing, we could be entering Scapa Flow.'

All thoughts of food have now left me. I'm just pondering on how very long a time an hour and a half could be. And I'm thinking about those wrecks, so many of them, German fleet and British fleet, World War 1 and World War 2, lying in that vast graveyard of the Orkney Islands.

I must have dozed off for a few minutes, when I wake to see Tommaso staring at the radar screen. My stomach tightens, and not with hunger. 'Is it a copter?'

'From its speed, yes.' He's calling Monsieur. I find a wall switch and extinguish the control room lights. Now our faces are lit only by the greenish glare from all the screens and gauges on the control console. Tommaso finishes the call. 'It's on Sea Eagle's radar too. Monsieur says to switch off all our navigation lights and put on full speed. They are doing the same.'

'Do we know how far away the Edinburgh is?'

'Five nautical miles.'

'I guess this'll be a Russian military copter with all the trimmings?'

'Most likely an Alligator. Fitted with machine guns, rocket launchers and anti-tank missiles. Top speed 310 kilometres per hour.'

His mobile goes. 'Very well, Monsieur.' He closes down the call. 'Monsieur says we must abandon ship if we come under attack. We use the rope ladder to reduce the height of the jump. We must jump outwards and swim hard to clear the ship, as she will still be moving. Once clear, we fire the flares. Sea Eagle will be on hand to pick us up.'

'So it's a doss, really.'

'The trickiest bit will be getting clear.'

'At least the rope ladder's at the prow end, not the stern where the propellers are.'

'There will be a huge wake to negotiate. I will cut the power if we are attacked, but it takes miles for a ship this size to slow down and stop.'

'It's 'when' not 'if', isn't it?'

'Spoken like a realist, Joe.'

'It's like Becks and me when the Alyona was sinking. Hope for the best and prepare for the worst.'

'There is another danger as we approach Scapa Flow.'

'Sunken and not so sunken wrecks?'

'Even in daytime, they are a nightmare to negotiate. I have put in the course Isla sent me – but this is a big ship with a deep draught and wide beam.'

We watch the radar screen as the copter comes closer. Then another glowing green dot appears. 'The Edinburgh!'

Almost at the same moment I say that, the sound of rotors overhead is approaching. It becomes a deafening roar. An enormous copter simply loaded with weaponry skims the roof of the control tower and lines itself up to fire on us.

'On the floor, Joe!' We flatten ourselves as a hail of machine gun bullets sends glass flying in all directions. The beast wheels on another circuit. It'll be anti-tank missiles next. Time to go.

Tommaso cuts engine power. We're out of that control room, down the control tower steps and onto the rope ladder more quickly that I would have thought possible. Tommaso goes first; scrambling nimbly down the rope ladder and making a mighty dive outwards to clear the ship. I'm hot on his heels. Hitting the water with a whack that knocks the breath out of my lungs, then swimming like a madman to try and avoid the wake.

The ship is still going at a hell of a speed and the wake catches me with ten foot waves. Coughing and gasping, blinded with spray, I hear an enormous explosion overhead. I don't think it's the Arctic Ocean that's been hit. Her massive hulk blocking out the night sky, she's going on her way, slowly coming to a halt. Could take ten miles.

A brilliant rocket shoots upwards, scattering shards of golden light. In the subsiding waves from the wake, Tommaso is treading water a few yards away. Lit by the fading sparks of his flare, he signals to me. Fumbling in my life jacket, I find my flare and pull the tag to send it skywards. A Whoosh, and more glittering gold fireworks. There's no sign of the monster copter, only the faint sound of rotors in the distance. No sign of Sea Eagle either.

Suddenly I become aware of the iron cold. It's inside my bones and my lungs and my brain. I'm not sure how long we can last in this. Then there's another sound from out of the night. It's the rumble of a mighty outboard engine. A Reinforced Inflatable Boat with a powerful searchlight is bumping and thumping over the waves at incredible speed towards us. My teeth are chattering with the cold so much that I can't shout what I want to shout: 'Blimey Tommaso – it's the Navy!'

Within seconds we've been scooped up into the RIB and wrapped in the same kind of heat-retaining, lightweight foil blankets that Isla used to save Becks' life. We're lying in the bottom of the boat and Tommaso's eyes are closed. I can't speak to him because I can't move my jaw. I can't move anything now. I'm not sure if I'm still breathing. Even my brain has frozen. The last time I felt like this I was with Becks in the Paris Catacombs and I'd been poisoned. I'm tumbling down those dark tunnels that are full of bones. Then it all goes black.

When I wake up, I have no idea where I am. Not even quite sure who I am. My memory has taken a hike. There's an oxygen mask over my face and a tube going into my arm. Next to me there's a rhythmical beeping that's echoed by another beeping somewhere to my right. I feel warm; not cold anymore.

That's when my memory wakes up and the whole Arctic Ocean drama slaps me in the face. I turn my head and look at the bunk next to me. Tommaso is wired up like me. His eyes are closed. With a shock I realise that the beeping is heart monitors, like Becks had after she nearly died in the ice cold sea.

A medic looms up out of nowhere, gently removes the oxygen mask and takes my pulse. He speaks with a soft Scottish accent. 'How're you feeling, Joe?'

The lockjaw has gone and I can speak. 'Is Tommaso going to be OK?'

'He was in pretty poor shape when we brought you two on board, but he's stabilised now.'

'Poor shape?'

'His heartbeat was very uneven with the hypothermia. But the defibrillator sorted him out.'

'Oh God.'

'Don't worry, Joe. You're both well into recovery now. We sedated the pair of you to give your hearts a complete rest.'

'It's just that Tommaso's twin sister had to have an operation … there was something wrong with her heart …'

The medic frowns, 'Then he needs to get checked out. We've been monitoring heart and lung function while you were both under. But it looks like Tommaso needs to see a specialist.'

'H … how long have we been asleep?'

'Twenty two hours. We've been back in Faslane for a day.'

'When will Tommaso wake up?'

'Looks like he's coming to now.' He goes round to Tommaso's bunk, removes his oxygen mask and takes his pulse; Tommaso's eyes flicker open. 'That's a good strong pulse. Now, we can see about getting some hot food into you both. There's jeans, tops and trainers on the bunk over there, and the showers are next door.'

As the door closes behind the kindly medic, I look for Tommaso, still terribly scared for him. He's looking at me, smiling his slight smile. He's going to be alright. 'You did it, dude.'

'No, Joe. We did it.'

The food on board the Edinburgh is so good, Tommaso and I are seriously thinking about joining up. We get really meaty burgers and thick, crispy chips with loads of T sauce. In the canteen, everyone who passes by says Hi and they all know our names. Two of the guys sit down and eat with us; they want a blow by blow account of how Tommaso hacked the Arctic Ocean. In return, we want to know all about this amazing frigate.

'How fast can she go?'

The crew member called Archie tells us, 'Twenty nine knots tops, Joe. Going at a slower average speed, she has a range of 7000 nautical miles.'

'Awesome! So, what happened last night ... I mean, the night before last? We'd dived off the Arctic Ocean because the copter had already machine gunned us and we thought anti-tank missiles were next ...'

The other crew member called Jim says drily, 'They would have been next. Did you hear an explosion, just before you fired the flares?'

Tommaso says, 'Yes – at first I thought the Arctic Ocean had been hit.'

Jim says, 'She's safe and sound here in Faslane with her very interesting cargo. What you heard was us firing at the Alligator. A warning shot across the bows, so to speak. Enough for him to realise he'd better get lost.'

'So how did you retrieve the Arctic Ocean?'

Archie says, 'I was one of the lucky guys who got winched down from our copter to take manual control. But yous guys had done all the hard work for us, putting her on a safe course and cutting the power before you got off.'

'And Sea Eagle? There was a plan for them to pick us up …'

'They were in close communication with us. We told them that we would be in a far better position to conduct the sea rescue. Knowing our ETA, they readily agreed.'

'So, where is Sea Eagle now?'

'Just take a look out there, Joe.'

Tommaso and I look through the porthole of the canteen. And there is Sea Eagle, gleaming white in the sun, moored nearby in this vast naval harbour on the river Clyde.

'Ms McDonald and Mr Rochelle are having lunch with Commander Airdrie,' smiles Archie, 'Whilst yous guys are slumming it with the likes of us.'

'Bet the burgers are better in the canteen!'

'Would you like another helping?'

'Er – yeah, please!'

'Tommaso?' He's up for it too.

Archie takes our plates. 'Yous guys have earned it, big time!'

While Tommaso and I are polishing off these wonderfully meaty burgers and crispy chips, Monsieur and Isla come into the canteen with a middle-aged guy who has piercing blue eyes and a very smart uniform. We all instinctively get to our feet. 'Please, please,' says Commander Airdrie, 'Finish your lunch. It's very well deserved. But before you sit, I'd like to shake hands with you, Tommaso, and you, Joe.'

I'm not normally the shy sort, but with my hand in the firm grasp of this man who has now saved our lives twice, I can feel myself going bright red. Tommaso is his usual calm self. 'It is a privilege to have been helpful, Commander Airdrie.'

'You have tremendous technical talent, Tommaso, and you both have great courage. You have served Her Majesty's Navy and our country extremely well. You and Joe are a remarkable young pair of commandos.' And there's this sound that I realise is clapping. The entire canteen, all these crew members, and the cooks, are stood up and clapping us. Isla and Monsieur and Commander Airdrie are clapping too.

—⚓—

The sea, for once, is calm as we four go aboard Sea Eagle and set course Northwards for Kyle of Lochalsh. So Tommaso and I go on deck to take a good look at Faslane, as we motor down the Clyde towards the river mouth. 'I bet they've got the Arctic Ocean well camouflaged – don't want Russian spy planes spotting it, do they?'

'The Kremlin will not be at all happy about it. Even they can work out that, if it's happened once, it can happen again.'

'I wouldn't mind a bit of a breather before we do it again!'

'All the same, I am going to keep a close watch on that computer in the Kremlin. If we can get more detailed intelligence, it could be that there will be no need for us to board a Russian ship next time.'

'We just send the intelligence to the Navy?'

'Possibly. It all depends on the quality of the data.'

I take the two bars of chocolate that I nicked from Sea Eagle's galley from my pocket and offer one to Tommaso. 'It would be useful to know where the Arctic Ocean was headed.'

'Have both of them, Joe – I'm still full of that huge lunch.'

'Well, that sleep was the longest time I've ever gone without eating.' I bite into the chocolate.

'There is just one thing, Joe, on your journey back ... keep an eye on your rear view mirror.'

'I'm likely to be followed? Who by?'

'The same organisation that tailed you to Bracknell. The Camorra established themselves in the port of Aberdeen some years back. They could well have you in their sights.'

'The Camorra are in *Scotland*?'

'Organised crime is a globalised business, Joe. It would have been the oil money that attracted them to Aberdeen. The Scottish police are having to do catch-up on an organisation that is very good at disguising itself in a cloak of respectability. Popular restaurant owner by day, drugs baron by night.'

'I can't imagine Lo Coltello ever looking respectable.'

'He doesn't have to. He's not the top man. Just the knife in the dark.'

Tommaso's words, spoken with such seriousness, chill me to the bone. The gnawing worry about Dad starts up all over again. And behind that is another worry: when is it going to be the best time to tell Tommaso what the medic told me about his heart?

The following morning, I wave as Monsieur's copter lifts off from the paddock with Tommaso co-piloting. The Bentley's all packed, the cottage locked up and the key posted. Just time to call Becks before I leave.

'Why didn't you call last night?'

'It was incredibly late. Didn't want to spoil your beauty sleep. How is everyone?'

'We're fine – how are YOU?'

'Just about to set off back. Tell you what, if I put my phone on hands-free, you can call me anytime and we can chat.'

'And you can tell me everything that's happened. All I got from you last night was a text on how good the food is in the Navy!'

All the way South to Glencoe, Becks and I do catch-up. We're still chatting as I drive between the mighty hills and running river of the glen, when the Bentley phone goes. 'I'll call you back, Becks.'

It's Tommaso, calling from the copter. 'Joe, you're being followed.'

I glance in my rear view mirror. 'By three motor homes?'

'By a black Mercedes coupe that is a mile behind you and has been tailing you for the last half hour. We can see it, but you can't. They've hacked your phone, Joe. You must switch it off.'

'Done.'

'Monsieur says that we must abandon casual phone calls and encrypt every message, until we are free of the threat from Lo Coltello.'

'And I need to do what they are not expecting, don't I?'

'Yes. Your route back home will be the same as Monsieur took when we were avoiding Azarov.'

So Precious and I take a diversion from the route where our pursuers would certainly have found us. We head for Stranraer, where we take the ferry to Belfast. Next, we drive south through Ireland for the ferry from Cork to Roscoff in Brittany. Then southwards towards Aix-en-Provence. And as the long journey back to L'Ētoile nears its end, I find myself wondering if there are still unseen eyes outside the gates of the château.

CHAPTER 7

Taken

It's two in the morning when I arrive at the château gates. When I call, to my relief it's Dad who's waiting up for me. The gates swing open with no sign of any unwanted presence. The sixteen point star in the porch is still shining its welcoming light. And there is Dad, opening the door, and coming out to hug me. 'You champ, Joe. You're a pair of heroes.'

'Shall I put the Bentley in the barn, Dad?'

'Not tonight. Come on in, you must be shattered. I've done you a pasta salad.'

He eats with me; I'm touched that he's waited all this time for his evening meal just so he can share it with me. And he wants to share more than the food. He tells me about how he and Monsieur first began to work together in the network. How far back their friendship goes. Some of the deadly situations they've been in together. We've never had a conversation like this before. It can't be easy for a secret agent to share his past life, even when it's his own son he's talking to. Because his entire way of life is secrecy.

I don't sleep well that night. The Mistral is blowing, and the moaning around the rails of my balcony unsettles me. I dream that we're back in the Corryvreckan whirlpool, and Becks has disappeared beneath the waves. And however hard I pull on the rope that's tying us together, she doesn't surface. And now I'm diving down, trying to find her. But I need scuba gear, I can't breathe.

I wake in a sweat with the duvet over my face, at half four in the morning. An hour later, I'm still trying to go back to sleep. But there's some dawn light seeping through the stained glass windows. So I grab my Italian revision guide and sit in bed with it, trying to work on the stuff we'll do next term. But I can't concentrate. Some nagging worry is gnawing away at the pit of my stomach. In the end, I shower, get dressed and go downstairs. The door to the Ops Room is ajar, there's a light on and I peep inside. Mum is standing there, staring at the blank screen of Dad's computer. She's very pale.

'What's up, Mum?'

'Your father ... he couldn't sleep ... said he was coming down here to do some work. But he's not here, Joe.'

'Perhaps he felt like a walk in the garden?'

'His car's gone, Joe. And he's not answering his phone.'

Hits me like a hammer blow. I'm silent, thinking of all the possibilities. He just went for a drive? Or he really has gone after Lo Coltello. Because he has the co-ordinates of that place in Napoli where The Knife took Gerda Budd and her chemist.

But that's old, out-of-date intelligence. There's no guarantee that Lo Coltello is still there. There's also no guarantee that he isn't far nearer than we might think. He could have had spies watching the château gates all the time. Like the flitting shadow I saw when I drove the Bentley out for Scotland. They were just waiting for Dad to do what he was always going to do in the end. Like a big cat, the Camorristo has endless patience: he doesn't mind how long he waits before going in for the kill.

'We need to talk to Monsieur and Tommaso, Mum, to work out the best thing to do.'

At that moment, Monsieur comes in, followed by Tommaso, as though some sixth sense has told them both that something has gone very wrong.

'He will be heading for Napoli on the Corniche,' says Monsieur, 'We will have to take a chance that they are not seeking to lure us after him.' Five minutes later, we're in the Bentley and the wrought iron gates are swinging silently open.

In the front passenger seat, Tommaso is trying Dad's number again. 'Still switched off.'

The sun has cleared the horizon as we hit the Corniche. The deep blue waters of the Mediterranean sparkle like a billion stars a thousand feet below. The road is fairly quiet and Monsieur must be doing a hundred, only slowing slightly to power through the twists and turns. And all I can see is Mum's pale, wretched face.

I feel a surge of anger: how *could* Dad do this to her again! But then, I can understand why he would want to divert the danger away from her and us. He knows very well they will be after him. And that's what he wants.

In a way, this was completely inevitable, despite all Tommaso's warnings. Tommaso himself didn't look surprised. With his quick mind and unerring instinct for reading character, he must have known this would happen.

Twenty minutes into our journey along the Mediterranean coast road, Tommaso says, 'There is a layby half a kilometre ahead. We need to check it, Monsieur.' And I realise that Dad is not the only prey that the Camorra have pursued along this road. As we slow to turn into the layby, a dread takes hold of me like claws. Because I know we're going to find Dad's white Porsche. I just don't know if he'll be in it.

Monsieur pulls in behind the Porsche. The driver's door is hanging open. The car is empty. All the tyres have blown. There's a single bullet hole in the windscreen: tiny twinkling pieces of glass are all over the facia. I can't see any sign of blood.

Tommaso says quietly, 'It will have been a double stinger. The bullet in the windscreen will have been fired afterwards, as their trademark.'

Monsieur says, 'We need to get out of here – this could be a trap.'

I notice that the keys are still in the ignition. 'At least we can get Dad's car taken back, Monsieur?'

'I am sorry, Joe, but they could have fitted a tracker or something far worse.'

'You mean, a bomb?'

'Yes.' He takes the key carefully from the ignition. 'We would not want anyone to try and steal the car and get blown up. Now we must go!'

And I feel as though it's the worst thing I've ever done in my life. Driving away from Dad's empty car. When all I want is to try and find him and bring him back. I know that won't do any good now. But I can't bear the thought of facing Mum.

As we hurtle back down the coast road, Tommaso turns to me from the front passenger seat. 'Joe, remember that Lo Coltello is not taking orders from von Schwarzberg any more. He is playing his own game now. I think it is most likely that there will be a ransom demand. That is the usual Camorra practice.'

'You mean – we could actually get Dad back? But do they keep their word when people pay up?'

'It is in their interests to do that. It keeps the victim available for another kidnap. A very lucrative source of income.'

Now I can hardly dare to hope. But Tommaso

spent a lot of time in the Camorra. Perhaps he was a lot more than what he calls himself – *a very small cog in the machine.*

Seconds later, Monsieur says, 'We are being followed.' I look behind and can't see anything. Then, I notice he's got the radar on.

Tommaso asks, 'You have runflats on this car still, Monsieur?'

'Yes, Tommaso. We have nothing to fear from stingers.'

So why didn't Dad take that simple precaution? But I know what the answer is. He's always been a risk taker. Always felt that luck was on his side. Whereas Monsieur only takes risks when he absolutely has to. And now Dad's luck is running out.

—⚞—

We're on an unusually straight stretch of the Corniche when the first rocket scorches overhead and shoots over the cliff towards the sea. Monsieur carries on driving like nothing's happened. 'That was so wide it was a warning shot. They don't want us to pursue the kidnappers.'

The second rocket isn't quite so wide. Monsieur's voice has a trace of irritation: 'Tommaso, can you take aim with a laser hand gun as soon as they come into view. We need to send a clear message that we are not a soft touch.'

Kneeling on the seat, Tommaso opens his

window and waits, laser gun in hand, for our attacker to appear. When it shows up, it seems that the Camorra have the monopoly on black Merc coupe's. Except this one has been customised with front-mounted rocket launchers.

Tommaso is a crack shot, as we saw in his spectacular defeat of the gun-runner Aquila in their shooting competition. As soon as the Merc comes into view, he squeezes the trigger. There's a flash as the beam fires and an almost instantaneous flash inside the Merc's cabin. The laser has knocked out anything in the German car that's microchip-controlled. Which is pretty well everything. So the engine and auto transmission will have gone into Limp Home mode. The speed-proportional power steering will not operate at any speed at all. And the electronic brake force distribution system will have defaulted to manual braking.

The Merc disappears from view. The driver will be wrestling with the non-operational power steering, massively heavy tyres and leaden brakes to bring the car to a halt: without going over the cliff down that thousand foot drop.

―⁂―

When we get back, Mum is in Dad's study with Becks. Tommaso says quickly, 'I am sure they will not harm him, Auntie. There are all the signs of a kidnap.'

Her face wretched like I thought I would never

have to see again, Mum says, 'Someone's sent a message to Julius' email. But it's all in Italian.'

Tommaso seats himself in front of the screen. 'It is from Lo Coltello. He says Uncle has not been harmed. If we do not agree to his ransom demand, this will change.'

'Dear God,' Mum's hand goes to her mouth, 'How much do they want, Tommaso?'

He gets up from the chair, standing in front of the screen so that no one can see the message on it, and looks steadily at Mum. 'Please understand, Auntie, that your husband will be back with you very soon. The price they want is easily paid.'

'You mean, it's not a huge amount?'

Monsieur says quietly, 'The amount is irrelevant. Whatever they ask for will be found, Nina, be assured of that.'

'It is not money, Monsieur. It is far easier than that. The Camorra want me to return and take up what they call 'active service' with them again.'

There's complete silence in the room. Then Mum sinks into a chair, shaking her head. 'No!'

Tommaso goes over to his aunt and wraps a comforting arm round her shoulders. 'Please do not be concerned, Auntie. I will come to no harm with them. I am far too useful to them for that.'

Tears in her eyes, Mum whispers, 'It's too high a price! I won't let you do it!'

Tommaso pulls up a chair and sits next to her. Monsieur, Becks and I take our cue from him and sit down too. Tommaso's blue eyes are bright, like he's looking at a plan that is perfect. 'Auntie, we all know that none of us can ever feel safe while Lo Coltello is at large. I will take my time and be very careful, and our communications must all be encrypted. But with me back again on the inside of the Camorra, we have the best opportunity ever to put Lo Coltello away for good.'

Monsieur's grey eyes look steadily at Mum. 'Tommaso can do this, Nina. We must be guided by him. He has shown extraordinary leadership ever since this threat began.'

Tommaso throws Monsieur a grateful glance and continues, 'I will be very tough with them about the handover. It must be in a public place where they will have no chance to try any silly tricks. A Catholic church would be ideal. Most of the Camorra are Catholics and this environment will subdue any tendency to mischief.'

Monsieur says, 'There are many Catholic churches in Aix.'

'Then perhaps we can look at them online and decide – I would appreciate your views on this, Monsieur.'

This seems to be a general signal for the rest of us to melt away. At the door, Mum pauses, her eyes still bright with tears. 'Tommaso, my dear, I don't know how to thank you for this. Julius doesn't deserve you!' From the fire in her voice, it's clear that she's very angry with Dad.

While Tommaso and Monsieur look at churches online, Becks and I take a walk in the garden. Corbo is on the grass, taking little dancing hops from one bug to another. Becks says, 'I can guess what you're thinking. Déjà vu isn't it?'

I'm seeing us sitting in beautiful St Mary Redcliffe church near the docks in Bristol. 'The son goes home if the driver comes back.'

'With that stupid journalist taping everything Bertolini's mate said …'

A far more recent memory is stirring. 'I think Lo Coltello must have recognised Tommaso when we were taken to that warehouse after we sent their cocaine to the Marseille customs officials.'

'But it shows that we're hitting back and they're hurting, doesn't it?'

'And they think that, once they've got Tommaso, it's all going to stop.'

Becks takes my hand. 'But it isn't, is it?'

I watch as Corbo takes flight and glides into the tree walk. 'I don't see how we can go on without Tommaso, Becks. He's been driving the whole project. He knows so much about how organised crime works. And he's the best hacker on the planet.'

She says quietly, 'Do you think we'll ever see him again?'

We get to the tree walk and enter its leafy coolness. 'Tommaso is the most amazing spymaster of all time, Becks. And remember, when he was in the Camorra before, he was a double agent. He tipped off Zeitgeist that there was a contract out for him and saved his life, didn't he? We need to trust him – I know Monsieur does.'

―⁂―

The Catholic church that Monsieur and Tommaso settle on is the Sainte-Madeleine in the Place des Prêcheurs – Preachers' Square. It's a sizeable church, around the capacity of St Mary Redcliffe at the time of our fateful meeting with Bertolini's henchman. So there will be plenty of tourists around who've come in to admire the stained glass windows.

In Monsieur's study, Tommaso briefs us in. 'I will insist that this is the venue where your father must be returned, and that the exchange must happen in daylight. But beyond that, I will let them decide the day and the time. In negotiating, you need to let the other side feel that they have control.'

'Will Joe's dad know what – I mean, who – the ransom is?'

'A good question, Becks. No, it is not in Lo Coltello's interests to let Uncle know what is the price. And so it will work like this …'

―⁂―

Lo Coltello wants the exchange to happen the next day at twelve noon, following the daily service at Sainte-Madeleine. Tommaso is to meet with Lo Coltello in a public library on the opposite side of town, and we will call him to confirm that Dad is back with us. Monsieur and I will drop Tommaso at the library and then go to the church.

Tommaso tells us that there has to be two, completely separate locations, because if Dad realises what the ransom is, he'll fight it. This way, he can't do anything to stop it. Tommaso explains all this calmly, concluding, 'The person who is going to have the hardest time in all this is Uncle.' I see Monsieur looking intently at Tommaso and I'm sure his thoughts are the same as mine.

The sun is shining and a brisk breeze is blowing as the three of us get into the Bentley. It would be a perfect day for a sail, if we didn't have other, more sobering business in hand. No one says anything – what is there to say? Half an hour later, Monsieur pulls up outside the library. Tommaso slips out of the front passenger seat. All he has with him is his laptop and his phone. They told him not to bring anything else. When I suggested he might like to wear the tracker watch, he shook his head. 'They will know straightaway and the consequences will not be good for me.'

Monsieur and I get out and exchange hugs with Tommaso. Dredging up some of my limited Italian, and half choking with tears, I say, 'Ciao mio fratello.'

'Your accent is really good, Joe.' He turns to Monsieur, 'Attends, à tout à l'heure, Monsieur!'

Then he's gone through the double doors of the library entrance. I stand staring at the doors like my feet have grown roots, unable to leave. Monsieur puts a gentle hand on my shoulder. 'Have

confidence in him, Joe. Tommaso is not the victim.'
And I remember Tommaso's words: *The person who is going to have the hardest time in all this is Uncle.*

—⁂—

As we park in the Place des Prêcheurs, Monsieur turns to me. 'Do you recall how Tommaso said farewell to me?'

'I've been thinking about the words he used. Was the meaning, 'Wait, and see you soon?'

'I think it was Tommaso saying that we could be hearing from him soon.'

'He's got a plan, hasn't he?'

'Tommaso always has a plan.'

The church tower is tolling midday as we enter the cool depths of the Église Sainte-Madeleine. A young couple are admiring a rich stained glass window, with its vivid Mediterranean blue and fiery red. Perhaps they're planning to get married here.

Monsieur and I take a seat in the front row of pews. And immediately I'm back in St Mary Redcliffe, negotiating that extraordinary deal with Bertolini's henchman. I'm so far away that it comes as a total shock when I realise that the person who's just sat down next to me is Dad.

He doesn't say anything, just looks ahead of him. In the soft light from the stained glass windows, he looks haggard and drawn. This is not the Dad I was with only the night before last. Then the awful thought strikes me: he might have been interrogated and tortured, despite what Lo Coltello said. So many terrible things can happen in 48 hours, after one well-intentioned mistake. I look round as a gowned altar server goes to tidy the choir stalls. There's no sign of Lo Coltello; he must be on his way to the library where Tommaso is waiting.

Monsieur calls Tommaso. He says just the one Italian word agreed with Tommaso: 'Riscatto.' Riscatto means 'ransom'; it also means 'redemption'. Something, I think, that Dad is very much in need of right now. *The person who is going to have the hardest time in all this is Uncle.*

—⁂—

On the way back, I drive while Monsieur sits in the back with Dad. I think Monsieur is quietly explaining what Dad has to know. Monsieur can always find the right words; like when he called Mum to tell her that Dad wasn't dead, but very much alive and on his way home. Now this is a homecoming of a very different kind. Because one of our number is not coming home.

I have an almost physical pain in my chest as I imagine what Dad must be feeling as he finds out what – who – his ransom is. How he must be beating himself up as he realises the full consequences of that one impulsive act of pursuit. How his dead brother's son has traded in his freedom and risked his life to go and work for the enemy. And how Tommaso may never again come home.

But I know Monsieur won't be putting it like that. He'll be reminding Dad of Tommaso's skills as a double agent and an *agent provocateur*. He'll explain how Tommaso sees this as an opportunity to bring Lo Coltello down once and for all. And he'll emphasise that we must all be prepared to play our part when Tommaso gets in touch. Monsieur will be putting it like this because he is well aware of how terrible Dad must be feeling. And feelings like that can be dangerous to the person who is suffering them.

Dad is a man of action. It was the burning desire to bring Lo Coltello to justice that drove him out onto the Corniche on that fateful morning. By sharing with Dad Tommaso's plans for communicating with us, Monsieur is giving him hope. And his wise words seem to let some light into the hell that Dad must be enduring. Because as I park up outside the château and we get out, Dad catches me in a powerful hug and holds me there for a long time.

For days after that homecoming, we exist in a state of shock. Becks and I carry on with college, but it's horrible travelling there without Tommaso. The worst time is supper, where the sight of his empty chair makes me choke up again as I wonder where he is.

Mum and Dad eat in their apartment on the

second floor of the château, and we see very little of them. Monsieur is endlessly kind and thoughtful, helping Becks with her Law studies for next term and me with my Italian. But it's like being in Limbo, without any purpose, just waiting and hoping for – we have no idea what.

One hot summer evening, Becks knocks on my door. 'I've had it with college work. Let's go for a stroll, shall we?'

Faint rumbles of thunder growl in the distance as we walk in the soft grass of the lawn, with myriads of bees luxuriating in the clover. Becks releases her pony tail and her red hair tumbles over her shoulders, fiery in the light of the sinking sun. 'When Tommaso does get in touch, how is he going to keep it secure?'

'You remember the wiki that Dad used to communicate with his agents? Tommaso talked about it with Monsieur and they've set up something similar.'

'So, it's password protected?'

'And everything is automatically encrypted when it's uploaded.'

'And decrypted when it's downloaded?'

'Yep. Plus his laptop has so much protection he can hardly access it himself.'

Becks crouches to look at a tiny bee investigating a creamy purple clover. 'I bet it's his hacking skills they want him for most of all.'

'Nobody does it better!'

Just then my phone goes. It's Monsieur.

'Tommaso has uploaded his first message.' Becks beats me to Monsieur's study – but only by a nano-second.

CHAPTER 8

Pirates Of The Mediterranean

Tommaso's first upload comes with a photo of an enormous container ship.

My dear friends

I am being far better treated than when I last worked here. They have set me up with an office of my own. I even have an Espresso Machine! And my main task is to be hacking container ships like this one.

In this case, my colleagues wished to know which forty foot containers housed a fleet of Jaguar saloons being shipped to the Sultan of Brunei. This was very straightforward. Stowage plans, showing where each individual container is stowed and its contents, are transmitted electronically as data files between ships and terminals. They are easy to intercept.

I was also able to tell my colleagues what time the ship was due to arrive in Napoli container port that night. This was because I had hacked the ship's navigation system. The easiest route into the system was via their satellite communications box. Most of these boxes are very old and have no security. Also, once the box is installed, the shipping company rarely updates the default access code to a better protected one. All I had to do was tap in admin/1234 and I was in.

When the ship arrived in port, thanks to the stowage plan that I had given them, my colleagues knew exactly which containers they wanted. They located them using barcode readers; the containers were then loaded onto waiting lorries and driven away. Just like when shoplifters go to Tesco.

Of course, we are not the only ones who are making containers with valuable goods disappear into thin air. It happens very often that the rightful owner turns up at the port to collect his containers and finds that pirates have beaten him to it.

They are paying this pirate well, by the way. How times have changed!

Ciao

Michelangelo

'Michelangelo! That was his father's code-name in the network!' Becks exclaims.

'He would have chosen the name as a tribute to his father,' observes Monsieur.

'He's good at this, isn't he, Monsieur?'

'His father would be very proud of him, Joe.'

Tommaso's next upload arrives the following evening. Attached is a photo of the port of Antwerp, Belgium.

My dear friends

This time, the target was two tonnes of cocaine and heroin on board a container ship heading for Antwerp, Belgium. I was able to hack the computers of the shipping company and re-route the ship to Napoli, where my colleagues' lorries were waiting to pick up the containers. The prize was worth 1.7 million Euros. And I have received a bonus for my contribution.

Ciao

Michelangelo

Becks twirls a lock of red hair thoughtfully. 'It sounds like he's enjoying himself.'

Monsieur switches off the desktop. 'He has to appear totally committed to his new job. Only when he has the complete confidence of his colleagues can he turn his attention to bringing Lo Coltello to book. That is the whole essence of working undercover.'

'Like von Schwarzberg thought Dad was onside, right until he was arrested.'

Becks says, 'Well, if they're giving him bonuses, they must be pretty pleased with him.'

'But never forget what a dangerous game he is playing. His life is on the line if he makes one slip.'

The third upload is also about a shipping firm.

My dear friends

You would be amazed at the resourcefulness of my colleagues in collecting income. This time, I was instructed to hack the finance systems of a shipping firm and plant a small virus of my own making.

This virus will then sit quietly and monitor all the emails coming and going from the people in the finance department. Whenever one of this shipping firm's fuel suppliers sends an email asking for payment, my virus will simply change the text of the message before it is read, adding a different bank account number. Millions of dollars will go into that false account before anything is noticed.

You know, it's hard to feel sorry for these people. They make it so easy for criminals like me. And yet it is so easy for them to protect their money.

Ciao

Michelangelo

'It feels pretty weird, Tommaso calling himself a criminal, doesn't it?'

Becks agrees. 'But what he's doing is criminal, though. It's just that the reasons why he's doing it are not.'

The next upload comes with photos of the front pages of Marseille's evening newspaper, Le Provence de Marseille, and the Napoli edition of the Corriere dela Sera. The one word headlines are the same: *Dirottamento!* for the Italian paper and *Détournement!* for the French.

My dear friends

As you can see, this hijack really made the headlines. From stowage plans that I had intercepted, I had identified another container ship carrying luxury cars – high-end BMWs, Mercedes and the like. This time, they wanted me to take complete control of the ship's navigation systems, and steer it off its course to Marseille container port and onto a course for Napoli, to an area where they could board and take over.

The ship's navigation system is not just crucial to its operations – it is also the most vulnerable to a cyber attack. It is based on an electronic chart display and information system (ECDIS), along with inputs from satnav and also the ship's Automatic Identification System, which tells other ships and the coastal authorities what ship it is.

Once again, the easiest route into the nav system was the satellite communications box. The default password of admin/12345 had not been changed, and so suddenly the captain of that ship found that he could not manoeuvre. You can imagine the panic on board when the crew found that an invisible force had taken complete control of their ship.

When they reached Napoli, my colleagues came on board posing as customs officials and 'confiscated' the containers holding the luxury cars. I was very relieved that they did not use force, and I did feel very sorry for the crew.

Ciao
Michelangelo

Tommaso's next upload is accompanied by an alarming photo of a container ship listing perilously; containers are sliding off the deck and crashing into the water, and the whole thing looks as though it could capsize any second.

My dear friends

I am beginning to have some ideas as to how I can bring about the undoing of what we shall call the Person In Question, or PIQ for short. He is planning to take over an entire car carrying container ship by stowing away, along with a handful of armed colleagues.

Once the ship has left Marseille container port, bound for Saudi Arabia, they are aiming to overpower the crew. They want me to hack the navigation systems and set a new course for the port of Durban, South Africa. Then, I am to cause the ship to 'go dark' – that is, make it invisible in terms of its identity and location, by disabling the Automatic Identification System and fooling the satellite navigation system.

I feel that the time has come to act because they will use violence against the crew, and the Camorra have never shown any restraint in this. Crew members will be ruthlessly murdered and thrown overboard.

Also, I can see an opportunity to nail our PIQ – provided that you, Monsieur, consider that the Marseille Chief of Police will be happy to involve his crack RAID officers. If that is the case, I will run my plan by you.

Ciao

Michelangelo

Monsieur immediately gets on the phone to the Marseille Chief of Police, receives a very positive response and uploads it to Tommaso's wiki. Tommaso's reply comes back in minutes.

That is brilliant – thank you Monsieur! So, here is

the plan. Because I can access all of the control systems on the ship, I can also make changes to the load plan and the ballast control. Both are critical to the ship's balance.

The heavier containers must be loaded evenly in the bottom of the hold. And, if the ballast tanks are not properly filled by the huge transfer pumps, the ship can develop a heavy list during a tight turn out of the port. This happened quite recently with another container ship; if the wind had not been in a favourable direction, she would have capsized.

So with this ship that the PIQ intends to hijack, I will deliberately put the ship out of balance. I will change the load plan so that the loading cranes put the heaviest containers at the top and on one side. This will create an out of balance situation that the transfer pumps will not be able to cope with.

On turning out of Marseille container port, she will begin to list heavily and the captain will have to stop. That is when the RAID officers can make their move. They will board the ship and catch the offenders and our PIQ before they have had a chance to do harm.

The RAID officers will also need to arrest me as well as anyone else who is here at the HQ at the time. Otherwise my colleagues will immediately suspect me and deal out summary execution.

I will send details of the ship, plus the co-ordinates and a plan of this building, directly to your email, Monsieur. Please let me know what you think of my plan.

Monsieur simply uploads: *A masterstroke, Michelangelo.*

But I'm looking at those two words 'summary execution', and thinking what terrible danger

Tommaso is in; with these men who would kill him without thinking twice.

—⚏—

Within half an hour, Tommaso has sent the details of the ship, the sailing time, the co-ordinates of the building he's in and a plan of the rooms and entrance. Monsieur gets straight onto the Marseille Chief of Police, and a battle plan is drawn up. The ship is sailing in three days time, so Tommaso must be already hard at work changing the load plan. Heaviest containers on the top, and on one side only, right where they shouldn't be: making the ship horribly top heavy, and completely out of balance.

It takes up to forty eight hours to load a container ship with five thousand forty foot long containers. So with three days to go to the sailing, those loading cranes are going non-stop. And the operators are blindly following Tommaso's bogus stowage plan, because that's what the plan says. They're all so pressured to get the ship loaded and out on time, that no one notices what's happening.

With one day to go, loading is still going on: and, after night falls, the man they call The Knife is sneaking on board with his gang of pirates. Finding somewhere to hide, which is probably not that difficult. There are very few crew on these huge ships, and they're all going flat out, making sure that the containers have been locked in place.

One third of those containers are on deck,

while the remaining two thirds are below the hatches. The ones on deck are going to need the most thorough checking. Badly secured containers are lost overboard all the time; the seas are full of them, and they can cause havoc to shipping. So the pressure is on the crew to make sure those on-deck containers are as secure as they can be. No one is going to notice that some very heavy containers are in the wrong place.

The ship is due to sail at 5.00 a.m. in the morning. Monsieur and I are up at that time, tuned in to the wiki. Two squads of the crack RAID officers, clad in body armour and wearing their helmets with intercom and cameras, are poised to go. One squad is in a powerful motor boat, waiting at the point where the ship – the Havana Gold – will have started to make her turn out of Marseille container port: and the list will be setting in.

The other squad is deployed in unmarked police chase cars, ready to make their move on the Camorra HQ. Here, Tommaso is monitoring the commands being sent by the captain through the navigation systems. If for any reason the captain doesn't follow the course he should, Tommaso is going to take over the rudder and steer the ship into the tight turn.

These enormous ships don't move fast when they're entering and leaving port. So it will all happen in slow motion. As the turn tightens, the heaviest containers that are all on one side of the deck, instead of at the bottom of the hold, will start to exert an unstoppable force of gravity on the starboard side of the ship. Slowly, very slowly, she will start to list. The more she moves into the turn, the more she will lean over. Tommaso calculates that she could end up listing at a 45 degree angle, with most of her rudder out of the water – so completely unsteerable.

The captain will be frantically operating the huge pumps that move the ballast water to the port side of the ship. But the transfer pumps won't able to cope with a list of this magnitude. He will have no choice but to bring the ship to a halt. At which point, the RAID officers will already be scaling the starboard side of the ship, half of which is underwater. The first thing they will do is order the crew to a place of safety where they can lock themselves in and stay away from the door to avoid gunfire. Then the RAID officers will flush out their prey.

And where will Lo Coltello and Co be? Wondering what the hell is going on, with the dramatic change in angle of the floor they're trying to stand on, for sure. Maybe even wondering if they can take advantage of the chaos. But when they realise that the ship is stationary, they'll know something is badly wrong. They might even think that she's sinking. In which case, they'll come out of their hiding place to try and save themselves. And find that the hunter has once more become the hunted.

It's Tommaso that Monsieur and I are seriously worried about. Once the RAID officers have 'arrested' him, he'll be in safe hands. But a lot can happen before that. Two hours drag past. Then an email arrives; it's from the Marseille Chief of Police and has two MP4 attachments which must be more helmet cam footage.

Monsieur opens the email. 'He says both operations were a complete success. Lo Coltello and three other Cammoristos were overpowered and arrested on the ship with no casualties. Five more Camorristos were arrested at the HQ. One attempted to flee in a car but a RAID officer gave chase and stopped him. Tommaso is safe, in a single cell for his own protection.'

'I hate to think of Tommaso in a police cell!'

'He is doing the right thing, Joe. If the Camorra ever suspect that he was the brains behind these arrests …' Monsieur clicks on Play for the first MP4, from the helmet cam of one of the RAID officers in the container port operation. And we're tearing across the sea in a roaring motor launch in the dim dawn light.

Ahead is the enormous dark hulk of the Havana Gold, leaning at a grotesque angle. In seconds, the launch is alongside the ship and grappling irons are thrown over her side. With unbelievable speed these six officers, in their black body armour and helmets, swarm up the ropes and leap on board. Two of them head for the control tower to get the crew locked safely away. Then there's a burst of gunfire. Lo Coltello and Co have come out of their hiding place and are going on the offensive.

For several minutes there's a full on gunfight. Then just as suddenly, it's over. Lo Coltello shouts 'Basta! Ci arrendiamo!' The RAID officers cease fire and one calls, 'Venez! Vite!' And The Knife and his mates come out from behind a container, chuck their guns and knives on the ground and raise their hands. They soon realised that this was a battle they had no chance of winning.

Monsieur clicks onto the second MP4. So, while the shootout is happening on the Havana Gold, two unmarked cop cars are screeching to a halt outside a villa overlooking the beautiful Bay of Naples. Six officers leap out, shoot their way through the locked gates, race up the drive and kick down the door.

Our officer takes the stairs four at a time and heads for a door that has been left ajar. And there is Tommaso with his laptop, standing up and raising his hands in the air. The officer takes his arm gently and they head straight back down the stairs and into one of the cars, with Tommaso getting into the back seat.

In the villa, there are gunshots. Then the officer's helmet cam catches a figure running down the drive and jumping into a black Merc saloon parked outside. Instantly we hear the cop car engine firing up.

The two cars are hurtling through the leafy Napoli suburbs at a terrifying speed when the helmet cam picks up a hand holding a gun extended through the open driver's window. The RAID officer must be steering with one hand and taking aim with the other.

He fires two shots into the rear tyres of the speeding Merc. The fleeing Camorristo tries to keep going, with horrible screams coming from the shredded tyres and the wheel rims grinding into the tarmac. Then he loses control, skids and the Merc ends up facing the way it's just come.

The RAID officer fires two more shots into the front tyres, gets out and walks in a leisurely way towards the Merc. The door of the Merc is opening slowly. 'Les mains en l'air!' shouts the officer. 'Vite!' When the Cammoristo doesn't seem to understand that 'Vite!' means 'Quick!', the RAID officer fires a shot straight into the Merc's windscreen. That gets the dude out of the car pretty fast, hands in the air. And it's all over.

Monsieur clicks off the MP4. 'Tommaso will be extensively interviewed at the police HQ, as there will be a great deal of valuable information that he can give them. The Chief of Police also says that, to make Tommaso's cover as sound as possible, footage of his arrest will be broadcast worldwide. He will also be handcuffed when he gets into the police car which will eventually – having evaded all potential followers – bring him back here.'

'What about when it comes to trial, Monsieur – will he have to appear in court to give evidence?'

'In sensitive cases like this, there are procedures for preserving the anonymity of the witness.'

It's early evening when a marked police car enters the grounds of the château. The Velociraptor has been sent back to the boot of the Bentley. The skies above the château are no longer being raked by the radar in the roof. Grandad and little Madame, Monsieur's aunt, are taking a quiet stroll in the grounds. Jack has emailed me that his band is still getting gigs, and he's going to be in Juilliard College, New York for a while. Arnaud and Talia have also thankfully missed all this, studying History of Art in Seville.

When the police car pulls to a halt outside the porch where there is a door with a sixteen-point star, Becks and I take a step back. Tommaso gets out of the back seat, his cheeks hollow, dark rings under his eyes and his hands still manacled. He looks thinner than I've ever seen him. One of the RAID officers gently removes his chains; they shake hands. Monsieur talks in rapid French with the other RAID officer. While Dad moves forward without a word and takes the exhausted young undercover agent into his arms.

CHAPTER 9

Operation Poseidon

The next morning is a Saturday, so we can have a long late breakfast instead of having to rush off to college. I notice that Tommaso is eating ravenously, attacking a loaded plate of bacon and eggs. 'They might have paid you, bud, but did they feed you?'

'Everyone in the villa fended for themselves. Groceries were delivered in a random way. Quite often when I opened the fridge, it was empty.'

'And of course, you weren't allowed out.'

'I was pretty well tied to the computer. But, apart from my criminal activities, it was time well spent.'

I pour him another coffee. 'How's that?'

He nods his thanks. 'There is a saying that you will be familiar with, Monsieur, and you too Uncle. Time spent reconnoitring is never wasted.'

'So you were able to do some digging of your own, while you dug a large hole for Lo Coltello?'

'Some very useful digging, Uncle. Into the Camorra's links with one of the largest drug gangs in Colombia, South America. I would like to share this information with you all.'

Monsieur says gently, 'Tommaso, you have been

deprived of fresh air and freedom for far too long. May I suggest that you tell us all about it on the Lisette? It is the perfect day for a sail.'

'I would like that very much, Monsieur!'

Half an hour later, we're wafting our way in the Bentley towards Marseille Old Port, with Dad driving and Monsieur in the front passenger seat. Dad never did get his Porsche back. It was blown up by the police in a controlled explosion, because of the strong likelihood of a bomb having been planted on it.

Becks is meeting up with friends in Aix to celebrate the end of exams, and I'm glad she's not part of this. I have the feeling that Tommaso is planning something and I want Becks to keep safe. I'm hugely grateful that she wasn't on the last mission; if Tommaso so narrowly survived that ice cold sea, Becks could not have done. Her life would be over and, without her, so would mine.

I glance across at Tommaso and see that he's fallen asleep, lulled by the whispering engine of the Bentley. He must have had very little sleep while he was a cyber pirate. What with the lack of sleep, hardly any food and the constant threat of what he called 'summary execution' if anyone suspected what he was really doing, he's been living on a knife edge for weeks. Yet here he is, with another plan for taking the fight to the enemy. And I still have no plan for giving him the news about his heart.

Tommaso wears a hoodie and sunglasses as we walk along the pontoon towards the Lisette: what Monsieur described as 'a sensible precaution' in case of prying eyes. Once we're underway and passing the harbour walls, he takes off the hood and the shades and gazes upwards at the Lisette's mighty mainsail with his slight smile. The sky is the deepest Mediterranean blue and a warm wind powers us through the waves.

At the wheel, Monsieur turns to Tommaso. 'Would you like to take the helm?'

He shakes his head. 'It is just so good to relax, Monsieur. This was a wonderful idea.' Dad comes up from the galley with coffees and almond biscuits. And, as we sail towards the blue horizon, Tommaso begins his story. 'You will all know about 'narco-subs'?'

Monsieur and Dad are nodding but I'm not. 'Narco-subs?'

'Once the police got wise to the high speed boats and helicopters that were being used to smuggle narcotics, Colombian gangs started to use submarines to avoid detection. At first, these were fairly crude devices which could not fully submerge, but they were still far harder to detect than boats and copters. Colombian gangs were ingenious at contructing their subs in the middle of the South American jungle, shipping in tens of thousands of parts. But then they got more ambitious.'

Dad asks, 'A fully submersible vessel?'

'And this is where organised crime became just that, Uncle. In Colombia, the drug gangs have no shortage of money. And in Russia, you can buy anything you like. What this particular gang wanted was to acquire a really serious submarine, capable of submerging to depths where it was completely undetectable: and carrying mega-quantities of narcotics.'

'A quantum leap forwards in drug smuggling, in other words …'

'Indeed, Monsieur.'

'So they went shopping in Russia?'

'The sub they purchased from the Russian mafia is superior to anything in the Colombian navy, Joe. It has a double steel hull and it can descend to 450 feet – completely undetected by the coastguard. Also, it is nuclear-powered – so it has a virtually limitless range without having to surface.'

'The ultimate stealth vehicle for transporting narcotics,' comments Monsieur. 'And what kind of payload?'

'Almost 200 tonnes – over one third of Colombia's annual export of cocaine. Enough to recoup the £7 million cost of the sub with billions of pounds in change.'

Dad asks, 'Is it armed?'

'It almost certainly carries torpedoes, Uncle.'

We're all silent. Then Monsieur says, 'Preparing to tack.' He swings the wheel and the Lisette moves smoothly through the wind, pausing only momentarily before the main sail fills with air again.

Dad says, 'We can see you have a plan, Tommaso.'

I can see the plan as clear as day. 'We're going to steal the thing, aren't we?'

'I think we can, yes.'

'But do you know how to drive this sub?'

'I have had some experience in far cruder machines. But there is someone in the network who has extensive submariner experience.'

I know what he's going to say. 'It's Daha, isn't it?'

'He has used subs on many occasions as the ultimately secure means of transporting priceless gemstones around the world.'

'It'll be brilliant having Daha with us.'

'I have been in touch and he is extremely keen. I have also contacted Zeitgeist as he has sub experience, especially sonar. We need four crew members so that we can have two on each shift.'

We're within sight of Marseille Old Port and the lighthouse. Monsieur asks, 'What is the timeline on all this, Tommaso?'

'From the data that I have managed to harvest so far, they are currently shipping consignments of cocaine from all over Colombia to the port of Buenaventura where the sub is located. We are talking at least a month ahead. I will know more after successive hacks of the Colombian gang's network, which I can now access whenever I like.'

'The sub is in a very secure location, no doubt?'

'Very, Monsieur.' He looks at me. 'You

remember the enclosed mooring where Black Dog was concealed, Joe? It is like that only way bigger – a vast hangar with a deep pool inside that leads out to the sea.'

'With guards who are armed to the teeth,' Dad comments. 'How will you get round them?'

'We will approach from the sea and swim under the hangar doors.'

'So you will need someone to get you to the mooring in a speedboat and provide cover while you board. Would you like me to be that someone, Tommaso?"

'I would be very grateful, Monsieur.'

In my mind's eye, I'm seeing us underwater, approaching the long black shape of the sub. 'How will we know if no one's on board?'

'I have already managed to hack her networked computer systems. One of them is the security system, which surveys the entire vessel from the control and command centre to the engine room.'

Monsieur turns the Lisette into the wind to halt her and Dad gives him a hand with the mainsail and then the jib. He starts the motor and Monsieur swings the yacht round and into the harbour of Marseille Old Port. Weaving nimbly through the crowded ranks of yachts and catamarans, Monsieur comments, 'What you propose is the most audacious strike ever in the war against narcotics, Tommaso.'

As Monsieur slides the 60-foot yacht gently into her berth, Tommaso jumps out to take the mooring ropes that I throw him. Monsieur continues, 'It will need to be meticulously planned and executed. And it will take great courage and resourcefulness.' He looks up at the young double agent with his half-smile. 'But then, that is what you are all about, isn't it, Tommaso?'

On the way back in the Bentley, his face tanned from the sun-filled sailing trip, Tommaso falls asleep again. I can't help being amazed at his calmness as he outlined the most outrageous anti-narco operation in the history of the planet. One that is going to make some extremely dangerous criminals a lot less well off: and very, very angry.

At this point, a thought strikes me which is not a pleasant one. I wait until we four are sat at dinner before giving this thought an airing. 'They'd better not find out who's nicking their sub and handing it to the cops, had they?'

Tommaso puts his knife and fork down on a plate now empty of a large helping of lasagne. 'Our lives will be worth very little if they do, Joe. So please believe that preserving our anonymity is the number one priority.'

Dad says, 'You're going to need one hell of a disinformation program, aren't you?'

'Yes, Uncle. I want this Colombian gang to believe that the crooks who have stolen their sub and its two hundred tonnes of cocaine are the Camorra.'

'Causing a falling out among thieves,' Monsieur observes. 'Because presumably it was through the Camorra's communications with this Colombian gang that you were able to access all this information?'

'That's right, Monsieur.'

'We will need to liaise closely with the Royal Navy.'

Tommaso nods, but I've not caught up. 'The Navy, Monsieur?'

'Once that sub disappears with its hugely valuable payload, the Colombian gang will enlist the help of the Russian mafia to try and find it. The Kremlin will be more than happy to provide warships. And whilst their sonar is nothing like as sophisticated as the British Navy's, they will stop at nothing to try and track the sub down. You will need protection.'

Tommaso's phone goes, and he leaves the dining room to take the call. Monsieur gets up. 'I will contact the Navy. The sooner they know about this project, the better we will be able to co-ordinate our planning.'

As Monsieur goes out, Dad pours me and Tommaso another coffee. 'You and your cousin make a remarkable team, son.'

'It feels like we've known each other all our lives, even though it's nothing like that.'

'That's what happens when the experiences you share are so dangerous, Joe. Living on the edge, you get very close to your brothers in arms.'

'Like you and Monsieur when you worked together?'

'Like Christian and I …'

Tommaso comes back in. 'Daha arrives at 7.30 tomorrow evening. Can we use the Ops Room for the briefing, Uncle?'

Dad heads for the door. 'I'll tidy it up – 'fraid I'm a very messy worker.'

I push Tommaso's coffee towards him. 'Is it very difficult to control a sub, bro?'

He sits and picks up his mug. 'It's a bit like driving a car – you have to be thinking about a lot of things at the same time.'

'Like?'

'OK, with a car you are thinking about what is ahead of you, behind you and to the side. You are accelerating or braking and maybe turning at the same time. But the big difference in a sub is that you are also moving in an extra dimension. Up and down.'

'So it's more like a copter – only under the sea, not in the air?'

He smiles his slight smile. 'I hadn't thought of it like that, but it's a good analogy.'

'So one of the issues with subs and copters versus cars is stability?'

'Absolutely. Directional stability, so you can move forward in a straight line. And side to side stability, so you don't wobble; although, with a sub's very low centre of gravity, this is usually not a major issue.'

When Daha arrives the following evening in the red Lambo, in faded denim this time instead of the deep blue suit, the interesting conversation continues. Tommaso wants him to give us all the info on the subs he's used to take his gemstones around the world.

Dark eyes glowing, he hands Dad a memory stick. 'Commander, this Power Point and MP4 will show you the display screens on the subs I use. Networked computerised control means that what used to be tasks for many crew can now be carried out by two or three.'

Dad brings up slide number one and Daha does a running commentary. 'Let's look first of all at how a submarine is built. It has two hulls, with the inner hull made from high strength steel or a precious metal such as titanium, to enable it to withstand colossal pressures under the sea. The outer hull gives the sub its hydrodynamic shape, and between the hulls …' he clicks to slide number two, 'Are the ballast tanks. Any volunteers for what these chaps do?'

Becks ventures, 'Filled with water, the sub can go down?'

'Precisely – and we pump out the water with pressurised air for the sub to surface. We also pump water to tanks at the front and rear of the sub to keep her level.'

The next slide is a close-up of short wings at the rear of the sub. 'These are moveable hydroplanes,' says Daha. 'Your turn, Joe.'

'Point the sub upwards or downwards?'

'Yes – and the rudder of course turns us to port or starboard. And this,' he flicks up the next slide, 'is what the driver sees.'

'Looks like a computer game.'

'Good comment, Joe, as all the controls are on joysticks. Push in to put a down angle on the boat, pull back for an up-angle. Now, normally submarine manoeuvres take place fairly slowly. But Tommaso will tell you what is happening here.' He brings up a short movie.

At first, I think I'm looking at an Orca whale breaching. In a massive rush of sea spray, a huge black shape is shooting upwards out of the water. Then it crashes back down on the water, disappears beneath momentarily and ends up floating on the surface. And it's not an Orca, it's a submarine.

'Blimey – can we see that again?'

Replaying the clip, Tommaso says, 'In an emergency, the sub can surface very quickly. It's called an Emergency Blow. The water in the ballast tanks is blasted out by air injected at massively high pressure, powering the sub to the surface. It's like being in a very fast, very noisy fairground ride. And if you're not sitting down, you have to hang on to something.'

Daha continues, 'The whole business of travelling underwater makes the nuclear submarine a wonderfully fascinating beast. It maintains its own air and fresh water supplies, and controls temperature – all, using the nuclear reactor. And the most interesting part of all is how you navigate without being able to see a thing.'

'Sat nav?'

'The Global Positioning System doesn't work underwater. Neither does radar. Instead, the sub uses a clever mechanical system, combined with Sonar – Sound, Navigation and Ranging.'

Tommaso explains: 'The sub can use sonar in two ways. Passively, by listening to what is going on; or actively, by emitting sound waves and listening to the bouncebacks from the potential target. The second option is more accurate, but it could give away the sub's position.'

Daha says, 'Torpedoes use sonar too. And I gather that this boat could have torpedoes?'

At this point, Monsieur calls us in to a dinner that I for one am dying for: brains use a lot of energy and mine is maxed out.

Over dinner, the talk is around travel logistics. Daha totally understands the huge need for us to remain anonymous on this mission. 'We will fly to Buenaventura by private jet. I am licensed to fly jets – that is how I usually do long-distance travel. I can arrange for a Gulfstream to be available at Marseille Marignane at three days' notice.'

Tommaso replies, 'I should be able to give you more notice than that, Daha. I am revisiting the Colombian gang's computer network later this evening for an update on the loading of the cargo.'

Monsieur comes back in from taking a call. 'That was Commander Airdrie. He has obtained clearance at the highest level for the Edinburgh to provide cover during your trans-Atlantic undersea crossing.'

'That is excellent news,' comments Daha. 'And presumably the Navy will want us to take the cargo to their Faslane HQ?'

'Correct.'

I'm trying to get a mental picture of what this undersea crossing is going to feel like. 'How many nautical miles is it from Buenaventura to Faslane?'

Daha does some quick calculations on his phone. 'It's 6708 nautical miles from Buenaventura, Colombia, to Marseille. Going to be several hundred more if we go to northwest Scotland. What speed is this sub capable of, Tommaso?'

'I hope to find out more about her top speed tonight.'

Daha taps into his phone calculator. 'So, let us be pessimistic and say she can do 10 knots. That will be around thirty days.'

'Thirty days under the sea,' muses Becks. 'It's a whole different world being a submariner.'

'Well, if you consider that we are travelling further than a third of the total circumference of the Earth, Becks …'

She nods. 'Quite a hike.'

Tommaso checks some data on his laptop. 'You asked about torpedoes, Daha. It looks like the Poseidon is armed with sixteen torpedoes.'

Becks loves this. 'Is that her name? The Greek god of the sea?'

'Greek god or not, I will just be happy if she doesn't leak,' Daha smiles. 'And it's good to know she's armed. That gives us a first line of defence should there be communications issues with the Edinburgh.'

I'm itching to know more. 'So, how are these torpedoes fired? It can't be like a gun!'

Daha explains: 'They are pushed from the launch tube by water pressure. Powered by batteries and an electric motor, or a special fuel that contains its own oxygen. And they're computer-controlled, the same way as an airborne guided missile. They use sonar to detect the target. Not as easy as it sounds, if you'll excuse the pun. There's a lot of noise going on beneath the waves.'

'And once they've found the target …?'

'If the crew are doing their job, the target sub will have noticed on their sonar that they're under attack. If it's too late to take evasive action, they may be able to deploy a bubble shell around the sub. This explodes and generates millions of bubbles, which make a huge noise and confuse the torpedo's sonar. So it no longer knows where it's headed.'

'But if they don't have this bubble shell – how does the torpedo actually destroy the sub? I mean, this is underwater – so it must be different to blowing something up on land or in the air?'

Tommaso brings up an image on his laptop. 'You are absolutely right, Joe. The weapons used against submarines do not even touch them – they explode beneath the keel. The damage is caused by a massive air bubble created by the explosion beneath the submarine. The bubble lifts the sub – or it may be a ship – and breaks its back.'

Becks says what I'm thinking. 'That is completely horrible!'

Daha asks Tommaso, 'Do we know if the Poseidon has the bubble shell defence?'

'I will be able to tell you more tomorrow.' Tommaso brings up a BBC News clip. 'In the meantime, you will be interested to know that the British Navy has a lot of experience in dealing with drug smugglers.'

The headline reads, *Anti-piracy ship returns to base*

The crew of Devonport-based warship HMS Portland has returned home after an anti-piracy operation in the Middle East and Indian Ocean.

The frigate clocked up 57,000 miles – the equivalent of travelling twice around the world – during its seven-and-a-half month deployment. While overseas the crew was involved in more than 30 successful anti-piracy and counter-narcotic boat raids.

It also oversaw the destruction of more than 50 tonnes of drugs. During one incident the crew intercepted two suspected pirate boats, equipped with rocket-propelled grenades and machine guns, in the Gulf of Aden.

Weapons confiscated

HMS Portland's boarding team of Royal Navy and Royal Marine personnel was supported by a Lynx helicopter, equipped with a machine gun and snipers, in the operation off the coast of Somalia. The frigate destroyed one of the boats and the crew confiscated all their weapons.

Speaking after the ship's return to port, Commander Tim Henry said, 'We came across 23 pirates in total and we disarmed them. We take their equipment off them and if we don't have sufficient a case to take them to prosecution, which we didn't, then we decide what they don't need and what they might use for piracy attacks in the future, and we destroy that and send them on their way.'

'Fifty tonnes of drugs!', says Becks. 'And when we first met the Edinburgh, she was just back from sorting out Somali pirates, wasn't she?'

With dinner over, Tommaso closes his laptop and gets up. 'If you will all excuse me, I will get back to my night job.'

Daha says, 'May I join you, Tommaso? It would be a privilege to watch a master hacker at work.'

'If you will one day show me how you cut and polish your diamonds, Daha.'

'It will be a pleasant way to unwind when this job is done, my friend.'

Dad and Becks head back to the Ops Room to carry on with the disinformation project. Left alone with Monsieur, I realise what I have to do, right now. 'Have you got a moment to take a walk, Monsieur? I need your advice.'

Out in the garden, in the cool of the evening, I tell Monsieur what the medic said to me about

Tommaso's heart when they got him out of the icy water. 'He said Tommaso's heartbeat was very uneven because of the hypothermia. So much so that they had to use a defibrillator to get it working properly. It made me think of Talia and the operation that she needed.'

Monsieur's face is grave. 'As they are not only siblings but also twins, there is a firm possibility that Tommaso could have the same condition as his sister. I will speak to Talia's specialist as a matter of urgency.'

'I should have told you sooner, Monsieur, I'm sorry …'

'I don't see how you could have done, Joe. The events of the last few weeks overtook us completely at more than one point.'

'He must have been under horrible strain doing the undercover work with the Camorra …'

'Thank God he got through that without coming to harm. I have the specialist's private number: I will call him tonight.'

At breakfast the following day, Tommaso announces, 'I was able to discover what class of sub this is, so I checked out her top speed. It is 28 knots underwater. More like 15 knots on the surface.'

Daha looks pleased. 'And the surface is where we don't want to be. A 28 knots top speed underwater is far more respectable than the 10 knots we allowed for in calculating the journey time. Could be more like 20 days than 30, assuming no problems.'

Tommaso says gently, 'There will always be problems …'

'Of course, my friend. And we will deal with them.'

With a feeling of unease, I ask, 'Do we know what kind of problems?'

Tommaso explains, 'Because we can't see where we're going, we will need to be constantly checking that there is nothing in front of us to crash into, and that the depth of the water is what the charts say it is. Sonar has to be our eyes as well as our ears.'

Daha adds, 'And in order for our sonar to work efficiently, we need to generate as little noise as possible ourselves. Especially as hunters will be listening out for us.'

'Then there is the question of communication with the Edinburgh. I doubt if we can use the military's satellite communications system. So it may be that they can call us but we cannot call them. Or, we have to use satellite phones and surface.' Tommaso shrugs, 'But this can be resolved through plenty of forward planning with Commander Airdrie.'

Daha asks, 'Did you manage to find out if the Poseidon has the bubble shell defence against torpedoes?'

Tommaso shakes his head. 'That will have to wait until we are on board.'

My mobile goes. It's Monsieur. 'Joe, if you could

drop into my study with Tommaso?'

He must have spoken to Talia's heart specialist. 'Monsieur wants a word with us, bro. Catch you soon, Daha.'

—⁂—

Monsieur has coffees waiting for us. 'Now, Joe, if you could start us off by telling Tommaso what you told me, about the time when you were both plucked from that icy sea by the Navy?'

As I start to recount what the medic told me, Tommaso smiles his slight smile. I tail off lamely. 'You already know this, don't you, bro?'

He takes a sip of his coffee. 'There is plenty of information on the internet about twins having heart problems. When I found out about Talia, I knew that I could have the same issues. I am so very glad that her heart operation was a success, although it took her such a long time to recover.'

Tommaso's laid back approach is driving me mad. 'But, what about you? You need to see a specialist!'

Monsieur says, 'I have been in touch with Talia's heart specialist. He can see you at very short notice.'

'I am very grateful for that, Monsieur. But we have a mission to fulfill first.'

Monsieur says gently, 'Tommaso, your health must come first.'

'It is very kind of you, Monsieur, and I understand your concern. But it only seems to be very cold sea water that causes a problem. Our dive in the Mediterranean went fine, didn't it?'

Another cold water incident jogs my memory. 'That time when Black Dog chucked us in the sea, you passed out …'

'And Arnaud saved my life, yes. I will never forget that. But the sea temperature in the port of Buenaventura in South America will be nothing like that of North West Scotland.'

'Bro, I can't stand the thought of what you could be putting yourself through!'

'Will you at least see the specialist, Tommaso?'

'As soon as we have delivered the Poseidon to Faslane, Monsieur, I promise that I will see Talia's specialist.'

CHAPTER 10

The Day After Tomorrow

On the morning of the following day, Tommaso appears at breakfast with a look on his face even more focused than usual. He must have had a very productive hack last night. 'I am building up a picture of how this gang operates. They work to a certain routine every day with the loading of the narcotics. Start work at 7.00 a.m., as the first delivery arrives. Then they work straight through until 3.00 p.m. and everyone leaves the submarine, presumably for bars and clubs. After that, no one seems to come on board until the next morning.'

'Giving us quite a large window,' comments Daha. 'Although we would need to wait until dark.'

'I also discovered that they will have completed the loading of the narcotics onto the Poseidon within nine days.'

Daha taps into his phone. 'Then I will book the Gulfstream for a flight from Marseille Marignane to Buonaventura, Colombia five days from today.

Her range is 7500 nautical miles, so we have 700 miles leeway. Not as much as I'd like, but she is the best option.'

I help myself to a fourth sausage. 'Is there food on board the sub or do we bring Tesco carrier bags?'

'From the data I'm accessing, they have been loading a lot of dried food that you add hot water to. Pretty disgusting, but it saves space.' Tommaso speaks with his usual calmness, but I'm starting to tingle. Suddenly this enormous project is becoming a reality.

On his way out to make the call, Daha turns, 'I will also organise the speedboat rental. We will need something very fast.'

'Zeitgeist says he knows a quiet hotel where guests are treated with great discretion – I will ask him to make the booking.' Tommaso gets onto his phone. I watch him as he makes the call to Zeitgeist. Hoping on hope that his heart is going to take all this.

With time on our hands, Becks and I go for a wander in the garden. She's excited about the progress she and Dad are making with the disinformation project. 'Tommaso showed us how to detect if our rogue computer's been hacked, and it has! So now it's all about building up credibility.'

'Like, putting genuine files that you don't need anymore in among the fabrications?'

'And encrypting some files in an easy to crack code.'

'So, as soon as we're on our way in the Poseidon, you start to steer the Colombian gang's suspicions towards the Camorra?'

'That's the plan. Only, how will we know that you're on your way?'

'Monsieur will be in touch once he's seen us off after the drop. But the day-to-day communications are work-in-progress at the moment. Tommaso says Commander Airdrie will tell us how it's going to work from sub to ship.'

She takes my hand as we watch the cascade of a mellow stone fountain with its silver music. 'You'll be far away and under the sea for a very long time, won't you?'

'It does feel pretty epic, yeah. But with Tommaso and Daha – they really know what they're doing.'

'And Zeitgeist. All the same – this is so huge, Joe.'

'It's that alright. And I'd be lying if I said I wasn't nervous. Mainly about letting my mates down.'

'You'll never do that! I know you won't.'

—ᴍ—

After lunch, Monsieur says, 'I am going to meet the architect at the Château de Montaubon this afternoon. If you would like a break from your preparations, it would be a pleasure to have your company.'

Daha exclaims, 'I would very much like to see

your plans for the new build, Monsieur.' Tommaso, Becks and I are right up for it too.

A very different scene awaits us from the blackened wreckage of the old château. The whole, huge site has been completely cleared, the plan of the new building has been taped out and diggers are excavating the foundations. The site manager comes over, gesturing towards the site office, where we all put on hard hats and hi-viz yellow jackets.

Then the architect arrives, and spreads out the plans on a table for everyone to take a look. These are quite hard to make much sense out of, so he flips open his laptop to show an artist's impression of the new château. And we're looking at a graceful mansion on three floors with large windows, some from floor to ceiling; the stonework is the same mellow golden as L'Ētoile. Extending from the left of the building, an elegant conservatory is filled with potted palms and tumbling, purple bougainvillea.

Daha gazes at the new château. 'It is very beautiful.'

Becks says, 'You were considering the idea of a moat, weren't you, Monsieur?'

The architect smiles and clicks to the next slide. It's a drone's eye view of the château and the grounds; and running round the perimeter, including the vineyard, is the moat. Except that it's so natural looking, it's more like an oval, joined up river; complete with stretches of rapids and small water falls. Becks grins, 'That'll keep the boars where they belong!'

Daha's dark eyes shine as he looks at the river. 'This is an idea that I may well borrow from you, Monsieur, for my house in the countryside.'

Tommaso asks, 'Because it is pumped, you can have fish in it, Monsieur?'

'Yes, Tommaso. And you see here, and here,' Monsieur indicates on the plan, 'we will be planting shrubs and trees to give shelter to kingfishers.'

'Kingfishers …' Tommaso gazes at the beautiful river, totally entranced. And I'm struck by the contrast of this idyllic scene with the deadly city of Napoli, where he chose to grow up with the Camorra; living unloved, lonely and in constant danger, to find his twin sister. Daha is looking at Tommaso as though he's sharing my thoughts.

—⁂—

On the way back in the Bentley, Tommaso falls asleep again. Daha says quietly, 'He has been through the mill, hasn't he?'

'I think he hardly slept or ate while he was in the Camorra HQ. And the strain of working undercover must have been horrific.'

Daha's eyes are thoughtful as he watches Tommaso's sleeping face. 'He has great courage.'

—⁂—

At dinner, Monsieur tells us that the Edinburgh has set off for Buenaventura, Colombia, South America.

'Commander Airdrie has briefed me on how communications need to work. He is sending you two satellite phones, with an emergency number and a routine contact number programmed into speed dial. You will communicate via the Inmarsat satellite system, which was originally designed to provide safety at sea with its global coverage. All messages will be automatically encrypted, and decrypted at the other end.'

He pauses. 'This is not the way the navy communicates with its own submarines, as they have their own advanced comms systems. And with the satphone system, there is one major drawback. I think you can tell us what that is, Daha.'

'As can Tommaso. We will have to surface to make and receive calls.'

Tommaso adds, 'This must be at night, otherwise we could be spotted by a spy satellite. And it would be unwise to attempt a call in stormy weather – subs are not very stable on the surface.'

Monsieur agrees. 'Exactly what Commander Airdrie says.'

'Presumably they will update Uncle and yourself on progress?'

'There will be regular communication ship to shore.'

'So, as soon as we are a long way clear of Buenaventura, and under cover of darkness, we will surface to make the first call to the Edinburgh. Is that what they are expecting, Monsieur?'

'Correct, Tommaso.'

'And during that call we will establish a procedure for future communications.'

Daha comments, 'That sounds workable. Are you happy with that, Tommaso?'

'It would be good if we didn't have to surface at all, but I guessed it would be this way. And we are very lucky to have the protection of the British Navy.'

Dad says, 'One further point, Tommaso. When and how is Zeitgeist joining up with you?'

'We will meet at Marseille Marignane airport for the flight in the Gulfstream.'

'Which has been booked,' Daha says, 'Along with the speed boat.'

Tommaso adds, 'And Zeitgeist has made the hotel bookings.'

'And your flight departure time from Marseille Marignane?'

Daha checks on his phone and replies, 'They have given us a slot at 4.30 in the morning, the day after tomorrow.'

—⚓—

Tomorrow speeds past so fast that I have no memory of it, except that the satellite phones arrive by courier, complete with waterproof cases. Tommaso and Daha inspect them closely and try them out. The satphones are chunkier than your normal mobile, and reception indoors is not good. 'So, we will need to be in the open air, standing in the sail,' says Tommaso. 'Another reason for only surfacing in calm weather.'

The day after tomorrow, in the chilly darkness of 4.15 a.m., Monsieur, Tommaso, Daha and I greet Zeitgeist outside the departures lounge of Marseille Marignane airport. Then the five of us are driven out to the Gulfstream in a minibus. Gleaming in the airport lighting is a sleek shape that will carry us 6708 nautical miles across the sea to Buenaventura, Colombia, South America.

Daha seats himself at the controls with Tommaso as his co-pilot. We passengers make ourselves comfortable – Monsieur, Zeitgeist and me. This really is a luxury jet, with leather trimmed seats, and a galley with a microwave and loads of food. There's even an Espresso machine, just like Tommaso had; when he went back to the Camorra on the mission that led to this one.

Tommaso is reading from a checklist while Daha does pre-flight checks. He signals to the ground crew and they remove the chocks. The jet moves smoothly forward then slows as Daha checks the brakes. Now he's talking to Air Traffic Control: 'Ready to taxi.'

Tommaso's voice comes calmly over the intercom: 'We are cleared for take-off'.

We're taxiing gently towards our runway; and the soft whistling of the two Rolls-Royce jet engines rises as their huge energy starts to build. The graceful plane turns nimbly. Now we're facing our runway, and the engines are screaming to have their mighty power released.

I see Daha's hand thrust forward with the joystick, and the kick in the back is even better than the Bentley. With a Whoosh that leaves my stomach happily in mid-air, the Gulfstream makes a massively fast dash at the runway: in ten seconds it's throwing itself at the clouds. I text Becks, 'Think I'm a jet setter now.'

She texts straight back, 'So fasten your seatbelt!'

My ears are still popping several minutes after take-off, so we must still be climbing. I turn to Zeitgeist: 'What sort of height will we be cruising at?'

'She can cruise at up to 51,000 feet but my guess is we'll settle for 45,000.'

'How fast is she?'

He chuckles, 'Very fast! Nine tenths of the speed of sound.'

'Blimey … '

'It'll take around thirteen hours. Plenty of time for some shut-eye after the early start.' He closes his eyes.

Daha announces over the intercom, 'We're now at our cruising height of 45,000 feet, so you can unfasten seatbelts.'

Monsieur gets up and heads for the galley. Twenty minutes later, bacon and eggs are doing the rounds, which Zeitgeist is more than happy to wake up for. Monsieur brings out fragrant coffees and sits down on my other side. 'What sort of city is Buenaventura, Monsieur?'

'A few years ago it was defined almost solely by

the cocaine. There were record numbers of murders and vicious turf wars between rival gangs.'

'And now – things are better?'

'There have been major attempts at social reform by the government. But this mission is directed at seriously damaging the cocaine trade between South America and Europe – and Buenaventura is still the centre of that trade. Even now, you would not feel safe anywhere other than the city centre.'

'I guess that most people are very poor?'

'Except for the drugs barons, yes, Joe.'

―⁂―

When I wake up from a long, full-bellied snooze, I can feel the plane descending and hurriedly fasten my seatbelt. Looking out of the porthole, I see a coastline with shores almost totally covered in jungle. In the distance is Buenaventura container port, with vast ships in a long queue waiting to berth, more monsters being unloaded by huge cranes, and mountains of 40 ft long containers stacked on the jetties.

On the approach to the port, on the coastline, I get my first sight of the other side of Buenaventura. In a jumbled mass are wooden houses built on stilts above the sea. They don't look big enough to be more than just one room. They can't possibly have mains drainage or a clean water supply or electricity. And I realise that I'm the opposite of them: the jet-setter. Nicking the Colombian gang's cocaine won't make the slightest difference to these very poor people. Just hope it won't make things worse.

I'm still feeling deeply uncomfortable when Daha and Tommaso make a super-smooth touchdown at Buenaventura airport. Outside, we pile into a cab and Zeitgeist gives instructions in Spanish to the driver. The driver rams his foot to the floor like we're in a Formula One, and keeps his hand on the horn, blasting perfectly innocent parked cars.

His death-defying manoeuvres include ramming a car in front that had the nerve to stop at a red light. But the car is such a wreck that the driver doesn't seem to notice, let alone protest. Zeitgeist gives me a sideways look. 'Welcome to South America, Joe.'

We finally pull up on a harbourside where dozens of yachts, speedboats and pleasure boats are moored. Zeitgeist enters into a heated discussion in Spanish with the driver about his charges and it looks like they might come to blows. Then the driver nods and they shake on it. Zeitgeist grins at me. 'They only respect you if you dispute the fare.'

'Right.'

Tommaso says, 'It is the same in Napoli; except when the car is not a taxi at all.'

'Then it's a kidnap?'

'Spoken like a Cammoristo, Joe.'

Daha leads us down a long wooden pontoon to where a sleek white speedboat is moored. It reminds me of Isla's Sheerwater. 'If you would like to take the controls, Monsieur?' Daha hands Monsieur the ignition key and explains: 'The hotel we are going to is accessible by sea as well as road. This way, we are less likely to be observed by prying eyes.'

'A good plan,' observes Monsieur. As soon as we're all seated, he starts the engine. Its throaty rumble tells us that this boat is going to be very fast. With Zeitgeist giving navigation directions, we chunter out of the port area at a low speed. Then Monsieur turns to Zeitgeist. 'We can open her up a little here?'

The engine suddenly roars, mountains of foam are chucked out of the stern and we're almost thrown from our seats. The boat is up on hydrofoils, doing a speed that is squirting blinding spray at my eyes.

Hanging on to our seats, bumping across the waves, we watch as the jungle coastline flashes past. This eye-watering progress continues for at least five minutes. Then Monsieur throttles back as we approach an inlet which houses a sprawling hotel and beaches.

Zeitgeist jumps out of the boat and tethers her on the pontoon, where a huge white catamaran is moored. 'Welcome to the hotel Maggiore.'

Daha asks, 'Is the boat to your liking, Monsieur?'

'She will do the job very well, Daha.'

Over dinner, we quietly discuss what needs to happen tomorrow. We have to locate the entrance to the Poseidon's mooring and make a trial dive to reconnoitre. We can't dive anywhere near the hangar or we'll attract the wrong kind of attention. So we'll need large air tanks and a very accurately planned course to swim underwater for a long distance.

Tommaso produces his new dive computer: the size of a chunky wrist watch with two faces. 'The compass is extremely accurate, so we won't get lost. Then, there is a pressure gauge that also gives decompression calculations.'

'Handy if you have to go deep to keep out of the way,' comments Zeitgeist.

I add, 'And we've got the head torches if it's murky down there.'

Daha nods his approval. 'Plus, we have brought the larger 15 litre cylinders, which will give us significantly more air-time.'

Monsieur finishes his coffee. 'Then let us make an early start. Tomorrow is a Thursday – not many bathers will be on the beach at 6.00 a.m.'

As I head for bed, yawning like an alligator, I wonder whether Monsieur ever sleeps.

At 6.00 a.m., stomach rumbling because the hotel hadn't even started to think about serving breakfast, I'm sitting with Daha in the back of the speedboat. In front with Monsieur and Zeitgeist, Tommaso is giving instructions, and we're on course at high speed for Buenaventura container port. Tommaso, Daha and I are in scuba gear; Zeitgeist will be remaining in the boat with Monsieur.

As we enter the container port, these monster ships loom over us like never ending cliff walls.

Daha points to a giant that is even bigger than the rest. 'See that one? Northern Star – it is more than a quarter of a mile long. And over one hundred feet high.'

'I wouldn't like to have to board that!'

'You and Tommaso did extremely well getting safely onto the Arctic Ocean. Especially in such rough seas.'

And I reflect, *Seas that came close to killing Tommaso.*

As though he is reading my mind, Daha says quietly, 'He has told me about his heart, Joe. He felt it would be unfair to keep it from me. I am very worried about him; but I respect his decision.'

'Becks and I feel the same, Daha.'

'The minute this enterprise is done, we will get him to the specialist.'

The engine roar is quietening now as Monsieur slows the boat. We're past the main part of the container port, and passing a row of enclosed pontoons. As Tommaso said, they're like the hangar where Black Dog was hiding in Kyle of Lochalsh – only way bigger. And inside one of them is the Poseidon, with its 200 tonne stash of cocaine. Above the entrance to each hangar, steel posts with pulleys stand braced to hoist the huge metal door. 'I wonder how deep those doors go.'

Daha replies, 'That is what we need to find out on this dive, Joe. We also need to discover what kind of depth the harbour is here.'

'Because Tommaso's plan is, we swim under the door and the sub leaves by the same route? Only, if we don't have the depth, we'll have to open the door ...'

'And exit on the surface, where everyone can see us.'

Tommaso turns to us. 'I have been looking at charts of the ocean floor around here. It is pretty deep – otherwise those container ships could never use the port.' He's gazing intently at each hangar door as we motor slowly past. Then he says quietly, 'The door with the eye above it is the one. Pretend to be tourists, we're on camera.'

As soon as we're out of range of the eye, Tommaso says, 'We're going to have to start at the first hangar and swim along them underwater, counting. The Poseidon's hangar is the twenty ninth, going from East to West.'

Daha says quietly, 'Let's do it.'

Monsieur puts on full throttle and the bow of the speedboat rises as we dash along the row of hangars, through the container port and back to the beach. Then it's on with the cylinders. 'These 15 litre cans should give us an hour and a half,' says Daha.

'If you swim near the surface.' Zeitgeist helps Tommaso to hoist the cylinders onto his slight frame. 'Because the deeper you dive, the quicker you will use air.'

'And last but not least.' Monsieur hands each of us a tracker watch. Tommaso straps his onto his left wrist as his right arm carries the compass and pressure gauge. Monsieur continues, 'You will not have enough air to return here. We will be waiting for you just out of range of the camera.'

Zeitgeist says, 'Take your time, nice 'n easy. Saved air is way more important than saved time.' Then we're tumbling backwards over the boat side and into the sea.

The water off the beach is crystal clear, with the sun glinting through the waves overhead. But gradually, in the long swim to the container port, it gets darker. Forty minutes later, a massive hull starts to appear ahead of us. Then another.

As we get to the third monster, its huge propeller suddenly starts to churn water. A pulsing vibration hits us as we flee for cover. Slowly, the ship's hull starts to move. With the enormous commotion of its departure, we're chucked around like shrimps in a liquidiser. And I find myself looking upwards in sheer terror at the hull we're sheltering under. Is this one going to move off too? If it does, we'll be torn to shreds by the prop.

Tommaso signals to us that he's moving on. In a cold sweat beneath my wetsuit, I decide then and there that I am never again going for a swim in a container port.

It takes an age before we're out of the port and at number one hangar. We have thirty minutes of air left. Pushing ahead, we steadily count hangar after hangar. And I notice that the doors go down only a metre below the surface. So, if the Poseidon's hangar is the same, all we need to know is where the sea floor is. If we have enough air for the dive.

As we approach hangar number twenty nine, Tommaso dives deeper; must be to keep us completely out of sight of the camera. Then above us is the door of the hangar. We have just fifteen minutes of air. Without hesitating, Tommaso swims through the entrance, switching on his head torch. Daha and I do the same.

The pencil beams pick out a black hull above us around a hundred feet long. It's lying next to a wooden pontoon. That's where we'll have to climb out in order to board her. We've found the Poseidon.

—ᴡ—

With ten minutes of air left, Tommaso pitches into a steep dive and Daha and I follow him down. I can see him checking his pressure gauge as he goes. Down and down. Ears thundering as we force ourselves deeper. Knowing that this is producing changes in our bloodstream and reducing our life chances. Zeitgeist's words echo in my head: *the deeper you dive, the quicker you will use air.*

Our torch beams slice through the dark, but there's no sign of any ocean floor. Just more black water. Five minutes of air, and still kicking down.

Then, Tommaso suddenly turns and signals to

us to surface. He makes a 'slow down' sign so that we don't do this too fast. Up and up. Trying not to kick too hard. But desperate now to get the hell out of here. Three minutes. Under the door to the hangar. Kick away out of range of the camera's eye. And there's the white hull of the waiting speedboat.

Zeitgeist hauls us on board and we tear off our masks, completely out of breath and totally exhausted. Monsieur slams on full power but he doesn't head back through the container port. The boat is jetting out to sea, up on its hydrofoils. Zeitgeist explains, 'We were followed through the container port. Had to do some fancy manoeuvres to throw them off the scent. Now we're not taking any chances.'

An hour later, we're back at the hotel in time for lunch. Which Tommaso and I are well ready for. I'm torn between Bandeja Paisa, which is apparently Colombia's national dish, and Fritanga. Bandeja Paisa is a huge food platter, simply loaded with protein and carbs. So you get grilled steak, fried pork rind and chorizo sausage on a bed of white rice and beans; topped with a fried egg, a sliced avocado and something called fried plantain, which is like a savoury banana.

The Fritanga is virtually nothing but meat – great juicy chunks of beef, chicken and pork and some more of the fried plantain. You just lay into it with toothpicks, no knives and forks needed. In the end, Tommaso goes for the national dish and I attack the meat: we share, and compare notes. And we have room for ice cream.

Daha, Zeitgeist and Monsieur find this highly amusing, as they play with their more sophisticated dishes; so I explain. 'The worst thing about these missions isn't the sheer blinding terror, like with that ship taking off. It's having to run for your life when all you can think about is where your next meal's coming from.'

Tommaso crunches the almond biscuit that's arrived with his coffee. 'We'd better make the most of it, Joe.'

'Oh, yeah, that disgusting powdered food that you add water to? That was what they were loading?'

Monsieur passes Tommaso the almond biscuit from his own coffee. 'Going back to your dive in the hangar, Tommaso – you feel that there could be adequate depth to submerge?'

'We were a hundred feet below the sub when we had to turn back, Monsieur. Even if there had been enough air remaining, we could not safely have dived any further. But according to the charts, there is a depth of three hundred feet in the surrounding ocean.'

'Which we could verify with an echo sounder.' Monsieur turns to Zeitgeist. 'Any chance?'

'I might be able to save you the trouble,' Zeitgeist replies. 'Just give me this afternoon to do some intelligence gathering.'

While Zeitgeist is out, Tommaso goes to his room to hack into the Poseidon once more and Daha goes with him. Monsieur has gone to update the Edinburgh on the reconnoitring trip. And I head for the beach, with sleep hitting me in huge waves. Veiled by clouds, the sun is just comfortably warm, and my head has hardly touched the towel when I'm out for the count.

—⁂—

At dinner, Zeitgeist still hasn't returned. Tommaso reports, 'They are expecting two more loads to arrive tomorrow morning – one of them cocaine, the other more dried food.'

Monsieur asks, 'Could you find any information on their planned departure time?'

Tommaso shakes his head, 'It could be immediately after the loads are on board – or it could be the next day. I could find nothing.'

Monsieur's voice is terse: 'Then you will need to take her tonight.'

'I agree, it has to be tonight, Monsieur.'

At that moment, Zeitgeist slips into his chair. I didn't even see him coming, this guy is so good at stealth. 'Apologies for the lateness. It was worth it though.'

'Did you find what you were looking for?'

'I've been on a fishing trip, boss. My Spanish was just about good enough to get chatting with some fishermen. I suspected that they probably had in-depth knowledge, 'scuse the pun, of the waters round those hangars. 'Cause some of the larger fish they go after sneak in there to hide.'

Daha exclaims, 'A brilliant idea! They fish there at night?'

'You got it. They don't want to attract the attention of the port authorities. Anyway, I had a bit of spare cash on me, so they were more than happy to give me a quick tour past hangars one to twenty nine.'

'How do they measure the depth?'

'They know how much fishing line they're paying out, Joe. They send the bait straight to the bottom, as it's large ground feeders they're after. Turns out that in places they've snagged their catch at three hundred and fifty feet.'

Tommaso breathes out, 'Perfect. So we can exit submerged.'

Daha passes over the menu. 'Better place your order, Zeitgeist. We're going tonight.'

The half moon flits in and out of cloud as we motor as close as we dare up to hangar twenty nine; leaving a good margin to avoid the camera. Everything has to happen very fast now. Wearing wetsuits and head torches, the satphones tucked securely away, the four of us tumble with just a slight splash into the water. The speedboat hull remains where it is. Monsieur has said that he will provide a diversion, should any alarms go off. Quite what that diversion might be, he didn't say.

As we dive and swim beneath the door, we switch on our head torches. Ahead lies the immense dark hull of the submarine. And we can feel rather than hear a quiet hum, which must be the nuclear reactor. Tommaso swims most of the way underwater, surfacing as we reach the hull. Then we haul ourselves onto the pontoon and head for the sail – the entry point to the sub; praying that it'll be open.

Tommaso jumps lightly onto the rope ladder coiling round the sub's bulbous sides. The heavy door opens inwards. We pile into an airlock where the door into the sub is open, and Zeitgeist closes the door leading to the outside world. It shuts behind us with a quiet clunk and he pushes home the deadlocks.

Steps go down into the guts of the sub. Swiftly, Daha now leads the way to the control room. The screens look familiar. He says quietly, 'We need to flood the forward tank.'

Seating himself at one of the screens, Tommaso takes a joystick and pushes it forwards. 'Flooding forward tank.' There's a sound of rushing water in the pipework running round the walls, and the slightest sensation that the sub has changed its angle.

Daha takes a joystick in front of his screen. 'Operating hydroplanes to point us downwards.'

Sitting at a third monitor that's making a steady Pinging sound, Zeitgeist says, 'Sonar's showing the door dead ahead.'

Daha says, 'Joe, you are in charge of our speed.' Another screen and joystick. He tweaks the stick a fraction and two gauges on the screen move slightly. 'We are submerging. Keep the speed at 7 knots.'

Tommaso reports, 'We've just passed two hundred feet.'

Daha responds, 'Flooding stern tank.' More rushing water in the walls.

Less than a minute later, Tommaso says, 'Three hundred feet.'

Zeitgeist replies, 'We're out. The door's behind us.'

Daha says, 'Rudder ninety degrees to starboard.'

Tommaso comments, 'Course is set. Zeitgeist can you keep close track of how much depth we have beneath us. I don't entirely trust these charts.'

Daha comes over to look at my screen. 'You can up her speed to twenty knots now Joe.' He takes over the sonar while Zeitgeist departs on a reconnoitring trip to inspect the cargo.

Zeitgeist comes back fifteen minutes later. 'There are suitcase-sized bales wedged everywhere. I've counted two thousand five hundred. Including inside the torpedo tubes.'

There's a stunned silence as we all register that we have no torpedoes. In that second, I realise that the rehearsals are over. We're hijacking two hundred tonnes of cocaine. And all Hell is going to be after us.

CHAPTER 11

The Deep

There's no time to get bored on a submarine. There are so many things you can't take your eyes off – especially the sonar – that by the end of your shift, you're more than ready for that powdered ready meal and bed. Bed isn't really the right word. Zeitgeist explains that it's called a rack, and that's closer. It's like lying on a supermarket shelf with a skimpy mattress beneath you and the next rack right above your nose.

We're wearing just the shorts and T-shirts we had on beneath the wetsuits. They soon dry off and we don't need more clothes; the sub is heated by the nuclear reactor to protect us from the deathly cold temperatures in the depths of the ocean.

With only four of us, we're working four six hour shifts every twenty four hours. Tommaso works with me and Daha with Zeitgeist. This is a routine that allows more time for sleep than the surveillance of Gerda Budd's villa did; and with no daylight to give away whether it's day or night, I'm amazed how quickly I get used to it. I sleep really well, because I'm concentrating so hard for every second of that six hour shift, I'm worn out by the time it's over.

On the second shift into the journey, staring steadily at my screen where our course and speed are displayed, I ask Tommaso, 'How long do you want to hold this course to Napoli?'

He's on the sonar and doesn't look round either. 'I think, a few more days. Uncle is putting out disinformation to the effect that the Poseidon has been taken by the Camorra. He is also in touch with the Edinburgh to explain our strategy.'

'When d'you think it'll be safe to surface and call the Edinburgh?'

'Monsieur will have let them know that we are on our way. So far, we haven't detected anything following us. But I would like to be one thousand nautical miles clear of Buenaventura before making any attempt at communication.'

We talk in hushed voices because sound travels a long way underwater, and someone could be listening. It could be another sub. Or a ship that's trailing a sonar array one hundred feet down. Everything is about listening. We're journeying like blind moles in the dark, with just our sonar ears to guide and protect us.

—◦—

I wake for my next shift to feel the sub moving beneath me. The rack above me is empty; Tommaso must have got up early. I hurry to the control room.

The pitching of the sub is so strong that I have to hold on to pipes and anything else to hand. At the end of their shift, Daha and Zeitgeist are eating some nameless substance with rice. Tommaso is looking at the depth gauge.

Zeitgeist mutters, 'There's the mother of all storms going on up there. We're at three hundred feet, but you can feel every passing wave.'

Suddenly Tommaso says, 'We're being pulled towards the surface!' The depth gauge is clearly showing the Poseidon being dragged upwards. Tommaso says, 'Two hundred feet and rising fast!' The Poseidon is now rocking and rolling like a football. 'We're ON the surface!'

Daha pushes his joystick hard forward: 'Operating hydroplanes.' The angle of the sub starts to change into a dive.

Ten seconds later Tommaso says, 'Forty feet down.' Then another monster wave hits the stern and pulls us back up. We're out of control and what's worse, visible.

Daha says, 'I have an idea. Flooding stern tank!' With the rushing of water in the pipes, the angle of the sub changes to nose up. 'Now flooding forward tank.' The angle of the sub changes to nose down and she's no longer rolling around. We must be submerged. 'Now get the speed up to 15 knots, Joe.'

I crank up the speed and within three minutes, we're down at 400 feet. Daha explains: 'We had to get the propeller below the water to get power back.

Waving around on the surface she was worse than useless.'

'That was very quick thinking, bud,' says Zeitgeist. 'Ain't never felt waves like those.'

Tommaso agrees. 'Most of the time, 300 feet should be enough to protect us from waves. They must be monsters.'

Daha says, 'No phone calls to the Edinburgh on this shift, then. I'm off to bed. We'll leave you two to keep the wolves off our back.'

We're two hours into our shift, doing a steady 20 knots, when Tommaso says, 'There's something huge on the sonar. It isn't moving. But I'm going to give it a wide berth.'

'If it's not moving, could it be a wreck?'

'Or a container. At first, they float. But then when corrosion sets in, they fill with water and sink.'

'Do you want me to cut the speed so the prop makes less noise?'

'In theory that's a good plan, because sound travels so much further through water than air. But this is such a noisy part of the ocean – currents and those monster waves – that prop noise will not make a huge difference.'

Half an hour later, Tommaso says, 'It is off the sonar.'

'OK if I make us a coffee?'

'That would be good.' Glancing at Tommaso's tired face, I conclude that he hasn't had a crumb of breakfast, so I bring him a couple of fruit and nut cereal bars along with the coffee. He devours them hungrily.

We're five hours into the shift, when he says in a low voice, 'We're being followed.'

'Is it a ship – or another sub?'

'I think it is a ship. I'm picking up the sound of a big prop.'

'A Russian destroyer?

'Could be.'

'How far away?'

'Just under fifty nautical miles.'

My heart lurches. Have the wolves found us?

All the way to the end of the shift, the steady Ping on the sonar continues. When Daha and Zeitgeist come on shift, Tommaso shows them our pursuer. 'We have to make contact with the Edinburgh.'

Daha agrees. 'Let's take her up a couple of hundred feet and see what those waves are doing.' Two hundred feet below the surface, no storm waves are rocking the boat. 'OK, a periscope look first.'

We go up a further one hundred and ninety feet and raise the periscope. Sighting through it, Daha says, 'It's nice and dark and everything's calmed down. Sat phones, Tommaso.' We surface, and they head towards the sail with the satellite phones.

Zeitgeist takes Tommaso's place at the sonar station and I carry on with speed and route. The

Ping continues. Zeitgeist mutters, 'They'll need to be quick. We're sitting ducks here.'

Ten minutes later, Tommaso and Daha come back from the sail. Daha says, 'The Edinburgh is around two hundred nautical miles away. They have our pursuer on their radar as well as their sonar – so it's a surface vessel.'

Zeitgeist asks, 'Any clues as to whose ship it is?'

'Commander Airdrie thinks it's quite possibly a Russian destroyer.'

'So what's the plan?'

'They are going to do active sonar – bouncing signals off the vessel to let them know they're being watched. They also have a Merlin helicopter that will do reconnoitring flights over the Russian vessel. Making it very clear that the British Navy is onto them.'

'Did you arrange a protocol for future contacts with the Edinburgh?'

'Same as the original – weather and darkness dependent. Now, you and Tommaso need your sleep, Joe.'

With the thought of the hidden hunter behind us, it takes ages to get to sleep. Then I dream about clouds of bubbles. And torpedoes breaking our sub's back.

—⚓—

When Tommaso and I take over from Daha and Zeitgeist, I ask about the bubble shell defence.

Tommaso nods, 'A good call, Joe. Daha, can we please check this out?'

Daha says, 'Let's start with a search through the menus on this beast.' It's on the torpedoes menu that they find the bubble shell defence. There's a switch for it in the torpedo bay that is full of cocaine and not torpedoes. Daha shrugs, 'Of course, we have no way of checking that it works.'

Tommaso agrees. 'Not without giving ourselves away completely.'

'At least the Edinburgh's on the case. She's more than a match for any Russian destroyer.' Daha and Zeitgeist eat some more of the powdered mush and go off to shower and sleep. Tommaso gazes steadily at his sonar screen and I stare at mine. The Ping continues.

With a stream of violent storms overhead, it's four more days before we can contact the Edinburgh again. This time, it's to tell them that in 24 hours we're going to change course. We won't be heading for Napoli anymore. The next leg is towards Marseille, to try and fool our pursuers before we make the final sprint to Faslane. Hoping on hope that we can lose that wolf behind us.

Twenty four hours later, the change in course completed, I ask Tommaso, 'How does the Edinburgh know that it's a Russian destroyer following us?'

'The British Navy has a very sophisticated sonar set up. The Edinburgh's hydrophones – the microphones in their towed sonar array – are linked to a computer database, which contains recordings of tens of thousands of audio signatures. These can be both biological and man-made; seismic – such as earthquakes – and specifically, the signatures of thousands of types of sea-craft. These include subs as well as surface boats, from naval frigates to fishing vessels.'

'Awesome. So can they set up the computer to recognise specific signatures and flag them up?'

'Exactly, Joe. The sonar operator can request automated detection and flagging of any number of audio signatures, depending on the threat frequency in that particular area.'

'So, the Edinburgh's sonar recognised the underwater sound signature of a type of Russian destroyer?'

'Identifying it from among a large number of other factors too, Joe. Such as the temperature of the water, its salt content and all the other ambient sounds in the ocean.'

'That is beyond clever. But we still have the Ping?'

Tommaso looks at me, his eyes dark-ringed from tiredness. 'I think we've lost the wolf, Joe. For the time being, at least.'

'So the change of course has done the trick?'

'For now.'

'Shall we let the Edinburgh know?'

'When Daha and Zeitgeist come on shift, yes.'
'In the meantime I'll get us a coffee to celebrate.'

―⚍―

Two hours later, Daha and Zeitgeist come in with their porridge breakfasts and we start to ascend towards the surface. We're at a depth of one hundred feet when Tommaso whispers urgently, 'Dive, dive!'

No one asks any questions when you get a command like that. Daha promptly floods the forward tanks and blasts pressurised air into the stern tanks. Rapidly we head back into the depths.

Tommaso points to a signal on the sonar display and turns up the sound momentarily. It's the unmistakeable clatter of a copter. He turns the sound back down and continues in a whisper, 'It must be from the destroyer. They've taken a chance that we're heading for Marseille and sent out their copter on our course. It dropped a sonobuoy and it was in luck.'

In a low voice, Zeitgeist says, 'And now we have no chance of letting the Edinburgh know.'

Daha whispers, 'We must try and work out what they will do now they have found us again. They won't drop depth charges or launch torpedoes – they want their narco-sub in one piece.'

Tommaso replies, 'The weather may come to our aid. My guess is that we'll have another round of storms in an hour or so. The copter won't be able to fly in that.'

An idea hits me. 'So how about we continue on this course until the copter has to return to the destroyer. As soon as he's off our back, we change course and head for the Arctic Circle?'

Daha and Tommaso look at each other and then at me. Daha says, 'Joe you're a genius – they'll never expect us to go that way!'

'Well, you know what Monsieur always says … you do what they're not expecting.'

Zeitgeist says, 'We need to check we've got the food for the extra days. If you can call it food.'

I can't help grinning. 'I'm the one who normally worries about food!'

I don't really want to go off-shift as I'm so keen to find out if the plan is going to work. But in the end, Tommaso and I grab a bowl of powdered soup each before heading for our racks. I wonder if I'm going to sleep but I go out like a light and no dreams.

When we go back on-shift, Daha updates us. 'We got the Ping back shortly after the start of the shift, so for a while we had two hunters on our back. Then the copter disappeared half an hour before the storms rolled in.'

Zeitgeist adds, 'We went down real deep before altering course. The Ping from the Russian disappeared almost at once. Those storms gave us some useful cover.'

'Feels like the weather might have improved now. Shall I have a go at contacting the Edinburgh?'

'A good plan. We'll remain on watch here while you and Tommaso go into the sail.'

We surface beneath a clear starry sky with the sea just a gentle swell. My satphone gets through to the Edinburgh straightaway and it's answered by Commander Airdrie himself. There's a pause after I explain where we're headed and I wonder if he's going to blow me out of the water.

His soft Scottish accent understates the seriousness of his response. 'It's a good call, Joe, given the hounding you're getting. But bear in mind three things. Firstly, while you're beneath the arctic ice, you'll have no contact at all with anyone. Secondly, it's remarkably well populated down there. Primarily with Russian submarines, of which there could be more than fifty: some with their nuclear deterrent, the rest, hunter killers that are protecting them. Ditto, in fewer numbers, US nuclear deterrents and hunter killer subs – who won't hesitate any more than the Russians to open fire. And of course, we have the UK nuclear deterrents and hunter killer subs, who will also see you as fair game. Finally, navigation beneath the ice is the toughest call of all.'

'So, it's a bad idea?'

'It's a great idea – if you can pull it off. Your pursuers will never dream you might take this route. I'll get the word out to our vessels and the Yanks about who you are and what you're doing. And there's some software we can send you that will help with the navigation.'

'Thank you, Commander Airdrie. Handing you over to Tommaso.'

While Tommaso speaks with Commander Airdrie about navigating the Arctic Circle, I gaze up at the skyful of stars glittering over the oily-looking swell. And think about all those subs from different nations, bristling with nuclear warheads. With their hunter killer protectors circling like giant sharks beneath the ice.

'Commander Airdrie is sending the software to help us locate strips of water within the Arctic ice where we can surface to correct our navigation.' Tommaso and I have taken over from Daha and Zeitgeist, and he's on his sonar station while I do course and speed.

'That sounds good.'

'Once we know where these strips of water are, we can use them to surface and correct our course using polar-orbiting satellites.'

'And communicate with the Edinburgh?'

'Yes. Also, Commmander Airdrie confirms that he has had our identity communicated to the UK and US subs operating in the Arctic. They do a lot of co-operative work in that area.'

'So we'll just have Russian subs firing at us?'

Tommaso smiles his tired smile. 'Commander Airdrie has also sent us a course that gives us maximum shelter from sonar. It is based on the software that measures ice thickness.'

'That sounds seriously useful.'

'The course is around six hundred nautical miles under the ice.'

The latest change of direction seems to have completely thrown off our pursuers. We were roughly half way across the North Atlantic ocean, heading for Marseille, when we changed course and started to travel due North for Greenland and the Arctic.

Once we're under the Arctic ice, we find water to surface, correct our navigation and call the Edinburgh. Then it's onward through the Arctic for the six hundred mile hike. Out into the ocean again via the Greenland Sea; past Greenland; and then Eastwards towards Scotland and Faslane.

That's the plan … Quite a lot depends on how many Russian subs catch us on their sonar. Tommaso says there are also plenty of Russian icebreakers out there trailing sonar arrays and dropping depth charges. The Kremlin has grand designs on the Arctic for its mineral wealth. And now that the ice is melting so fast, they also want to set up trade routes which ships must pay to use. So they're not exactly going to roll out the red carpet for us.

CHAPTER 12

Fire And Ice

I can't remember how long it took to reach the Arctic; one shift just blurred into the next. No one cared anymore what day or date or month it was. But I do remember that not once on our new course did we get any nerve-wracking Pings.

Tommaso seemed to relax a bit and his eyes looked less tired; I made sure he ate more often, too. Then came the unforgettable shift when we arrived to take over and Zeitgeist announced in his gruff voice, 'We got ice for a ceiling, dudes.'

Tommaso sits down in front of the sonar and I can see his jaw tensing up. Daha says, 'I'll bring you both some cereal bars and coffee.'

Five hours into the shift, Tommaso stares at something on his screen. 'We're under attack, Joe. Launch the bubble shell!'

Racing into the torpedo bay, I hit the bubble shell switch. Nothing happens. I tear back to the control room. 'It's not working!'

Tommaso points at the screen. 'Something's working. The torpedo disappeared in one big bang.'

'But we didn't fire at them.'

'No, but someone did. We have powerful friends down here, Joe.'

'It must be Commander Airdrie – telling our subs and the Yanks about who we are and what we're doing.'

'And whoever it is, American or British, they have anti-torpedo torpedoes.'

My legs suddenly feel weak with relief and I sit down at my screen. 'Beats that bloody bubble shell!'

Nothing else eventful occurs on our shift. Daha and Zeitgeist stare in stunned amazement as Tommaso explains what happened while they were sleeping. Zeitgeist raises his coffee in a toast, 'Here's to the smoking gun!'

We didn't exactly get used to being rescued from attacking torpedoes on twenty two occasions during that trip. We still held our breath when the sonar picked up another lethal cylinder snaking its way towards us. But whether they were from American or British subs, the anti-torpedo torpedoes worked with clinical precision. Making it pretty obvious who our attackers were. Time after time, another torpedo would appear on the sonar; only to be blown up by our allies beneath the ice.

Now the urgent need is to communicate with the Edinburgh. Tommaso is closely monitoring the software that will guide us to water where we can surface. Daha and Zeitgeist have cut short their sleep in order to be on hand for this critical manoeuvre. Half an hour later, Tommaso says, 'We can start to surface, very gradually.'

Daha begins to blast air into the forward tank. We can feel the slight tilt upwards. We've gone from four hundred to two hundred feet depth, when Tommaso says, 'We need to make it more gradual now, as the software does not operate in real time.'

'You mean, it could have frozen over up there?'

'Yes. If it is ice, we need to contact with it as gently as possible. The British and US subs have upward looking sonar that can assess ice thickness. And they have a hardened sail that can push up through ice. I would not want to chance anything like that with this sub.'

'So, if it's ice, we try again somewhere else?'

'I hope very much that it's water, because we must re-establish contact with the Edinburgh. OK, checking that the periscope is completely retracted. Can you level us out now, Daha?' Daha blasts air into the stern tank and the sub returns to a level attitude, perfectly balanced fore and aft. We hold our breath, dreading the impact overhead if the water has turned into ice.

But mercifully, no impact happens. Daha raises the periscope. 'That was beautifully done, my friend! Now, we will need to put on wetsuits and spend minimal time in the freezing air.'

Tommaso says, 'I will remain on station – someone needs to.'

I can see the relief on Daha's face and I'm feeling it too.

Nothing can prepare you for your first sight of the Arctic. The dazzling white wastes go relentlessly on all around you; your eyes ache with the whiteness. The total silence and the leaden sky weigh you down. And the cold will kill you in a very short time if all you have to protect you is a wetsuit.

With our fingers rapidly going completely numb, Zeitgeist and I busy ourselves checking navigation with the polar-orbiting satellites, while Daha calls Commander Airdrie. Then it's back down into the warmth of the sub. This is not a place where you take selfies.

We get quickly underway again. I make Tommaso and myself some kind of rice mush before we turn in. Daha says, 'Commander Airdrie says the Edinburgh will be waiting at the point where we are due to exit the ice into the Greenland Sea.'

'Did you ask him about who's been protecting us?'

He shakes his head with a smile. 'He would not have been allowed to tell us, Joe. That kind of information is classified.'

'Then I'll put my money on a joint effort.'

'Commander Airdrie also warned us to keep as southwards a course as possible.'

'Why's that?'

'He says that underwater volcanic eruptions have been occurring beneath the Arctic for the last three months. If we get caught up in one, it could seriously damage the Poseidon.'

'Right. We'll sleep on it – good luck, dudes.'

—✠—

Tommaso and I don't sleep on it for very long. The first thing I remember is both of us being thrown violently out of our racks. Then one of the cocaine bales topples out of the third rack above us and lands on my face.

We stumble into the command room. Daha is frowning with concentration. 'We're passing through an underwater eruption. I'm trying to get her nearer the surface but it's not easy.'

At the sonar, Zeitgeist growls, 'There's nothing to see and there's too much to see – it's like the goddam wood and the trees!'

Half an hour later, Daha manages to get us from 400 feet to 150 feet below the ice, and the manic pitching and rolling calms down a bit. 'Joe, can you take over here while I check for damage? She's taken an awful beating.'

He comes back in just a few minutes, his face grave. 'I'm afraid we have a leak in the torpedo bay. One of the valves …'

'Can we pump it out?'

'For the time being, yes. But if it gets worse …'

Tommaso says, 'If I take over on the sonar, maybe

you and Zeitgeist together could attempt a fix? There's a toolbox and patching materials in the bay.'

Zeitgeist gets up. 'Worth a try.' He and Daha head for the torpedo bay.

I look at Tommaso. 'Full speed ahead?'

'Yes, it's time to make a run for it, Joe. We have to get out of the ice.'

I crank the speed up to the Poseidon's 28 knots maximum. At this rate of progress, Tommaso must be having a dizzying time on the sonar. If we crash into something now, it'll cause massive damage to the prow where the sonar microphones are located. Then we'll be in a sub that can't hear a thing and can't surface either. I wonder if our undersea guardians are still looking out for us. After that rough and tumble ride through the eruptions, we may never know.

—⁂—

Around an hour later, Daha and Zeitgeist come back from the torpedo bay soaking wet, cold and frustrated. Zeitgeist shakes his head. 'Ain't no deal, bud.'

Daha explains, 'We can't isolate the valve to replace it while we're underwater. And the leak's getting worse.'

Tommaso checks with the software that Commander Airdrie sent us. 'Another twenty two nautical miles and we're out of the ice.' He looks at me.

I do some quick sums in my head. 'At this speed – around 47 minutes.'

'Jeez,' Zeitgeist grimaces.

Daha says suddenly, 'How deep are we?'

'Still running at a hundred and fifty feet.'

'If we can cut that by even twenty feet, it'll reduce the pressure on the hull. Could make a difference to the rate the water's coming in.'

Tommaso frowns, 'That would take us dangerously close to pressure ridges in the ice crust. If we hit one at top speed, we're all dead.'

Daha nods in agreement. 'You're right, of course; there have been pressure ridges recorded at more than 150 feet down. But if we don't slow this leak …'

Zeitgeist mutters, 'Between a rock and a hard place …'

Tommaso says, 'We'll go to 130 feet and see if it makes a difference to the leak.'

'A good plan,' Daha replies. 'And the second we're out of the ice we do an emergency blow.'

'Surely we need to go up slowly in case there's a ship on the surface?'

'We won't have the time, Joe. By then the leak could be threatening to drag this sub to the bottom and we'll be swimming.' We all look at the switch that will carry us to the surface in a matter of seconds. Then I get back to my screen, Tommaso locks back on to his sonar and Daha and Zeitgeist return to the torpedo bay.

For the next twenty minutes, Tommaso and I are both sweating with the strain but we manage not to hit anything. Zeitgeist reports back. 'If anything it's gotten worse. So head back down again guys.' Relieved, we flood the forward ballast tank and point the Poseidon's nose downwards, away from those deadly pressure ridges.

Half an hour later, Tommaso checks the ice locator software again. 'We're almost clear.'

Zeitgeist and Daha come in from the torpedo bay. 'How far now, Tommaso?'

'Five hundred metres, Daha.'

And now I'm starting to feel really nervous about this emergency blow. Suppose it doesn't work? The bubble shell defence didn't. Or suppose we hit a ship?

Tommaso says quietly, 'We're out.'

Daha hits the switch. Instantly there's a deafening hissing of air through the pipes and the sub changes to a steep up angle. Zeitgeist has been holding onto a pipe and he lets go suddenly, 'Jeez it's freezing!'

Now we can feel a colossal pull of gravity as we shoot upwards like a rocket. Please don't let there be anything above us! Not ice, not a boat! We're hanging on with all our might as this gigantic fairground ride powers towards the surface of the Arctic Sea. Then we must have broken surface, because the angle changes, levelling out.

Now my stomach gets left behind as the sub

crashes down onto the surface. In my mind's eye I'm replaying the video, watching her sink slightly before settling on the water.

Daha raises the periscope. Zeitgeist says breathlessly, 'Can you see anything, bud?'

Daha smiles his most brilliant smile. 'I can see a sight for sore eyes, my friends.'

He motions me to take a look. And there's the RIB from the Edinburgh charging across the choppy waves towards us. A full complement of marines is on board, bristling for action. Behind them is the frigate. And just at that moment, icy salt water from the torpedo bay gushes into the control room and swirls round our feet.

With the water level rising, it's a mad struggle into the wetsuits and up into the sail. There we come face to face with six marines who've boarded while we were wrestling with zips. Even with the wetsuits, the shock of cold air is paralysing and I'm terrified for Tommaso.

Daha quickly explains about the leak and three marines go below to sort it out while the others rush us into the RIB. There they wrap us all in foil blankets while the helm puts on full speed back to the Edinburgh. Tommaso's face is very pale and his eyes are closed. I remember thinking, 'No, it can't end like this. It mustn't!'

The medics take Tommaso on a stretcher straight to the Edinburgh's emergency treatment bay. The rest of us are given warm clothes and served hot food in the canteen. But all I can think about is Tommaso and his failing heart. Daha is toying with his food in a way that says he's thinking the same thoughts.

Suddenly alarms are going off and everyone in the canteen gets up and runs out the door. Jim and Archie are among them. Archie throws a brief comment our way. 'We're being buzzed by seventeen Russian fighters!' Looking out of the portholes, we can see them.

Daha exclaims, 'Flying as low as that, they'll have their electronics scrambled by the Edinburgh's radar system!'

'Do you think they're after the Poseidon?'

Zeitgeist says, 'Probably not. Russia thinks it owns the entire Arctic. It has a load of military bases there and it likes to warn people off.'

'Seventeen fighters is a lot!'

Daha replies, 'They have no idea what they're up against with a Royal Navy frigate, Joe. The Edinburgh probably has forty eight missiles so I think we'd win that round.'

I'm staring at the doorway, where someone I know is coming in and giving me a small wave. 'I think Tommaso's won his round too.'

The rest of the journey back to Faslane is uneventful, apart from a severe storm as we rounded Cape Wrath and entered the Minch. Even the marines navigating the Poseidon must have felt those towering waves. But the Edinburgh just sailed masterfully on through all the weather.

Shortly before we're due to set off from Faslane to travel home, Commander Airdrie invites us all into his wood-panelled cabin. Some extremely good coffee is lined up for us and a plateful of very chocolatey biscuits.

'What you four commandos have achieved is the most resounding blow ever dealt to the narcotics trade. Normally, the Navy makes its drugs seizures very public. But I respect the overwhelming need to keep your identities secret. And besides, this was your achievement: the Navy simply provided back-up.'

Daha responds, 'Back-up that saved our lives once again, Commander Airdrie.'

'Just doing our job, Daha. Now, please carry with you the knowledge that Her Majesty's government is forever in your debt.' He looks at Tommaso. 'And very possibly we could be working together again – remotely, this time.'

Tommaso smiles his slight smile. 'There is still a rich vein of intelligence to be mined, Commander Airdrie. I look forward to it.'

CHAPTER 13

Kingfishers

Zeitgeist melted away from Faslane like the skilled agent he is. The Navy flew the rest of us all the way back to L'Ētoile in a huge Merlin helicopter. I just sat there staring out at the sky, thinking how beautiful the clouds were and how lucky I was to be able to see them again. And I kept looking round at Tommaso; feeling this massive thankfulness that he was still with us.

He said it was a simple case of low blood sugar that made him pass out. The chips and burgers in the Edinburgh's canteen soon sorted that out. Tasted like heaven after weeks of that horrible mush on the Poseidon. And for the trip back, Jim and Archie gave us a boxload of Mars bars to keep everyone going. They waved us Goodbye as the Merlin lifted off with its mighty rotors thundering. I looked down at the grey waters of the vast naval harbour and wondered what they'd done with the sub and its toxic cargo.

Up here in the Scottish skies, the memory of our time beneath the sea is a blur. I still have no idea what day of the week it is or even what month. Don't really care. I'm just glad that we're all alive.

As soon as we got back to L'Étoile, Monsieur contacted Talia's heart specialist and made an appointment for Tommaso. But then something happened which changed everything.

Becks and I are sitting having breakfast with Mum and Dad, and he's explaining to me just how long we were all in that submarine, when Tommaso comes in with Daha and Monsieur. They're all looking so serious that the room goes completely silent.

Tommaso says quietly, 'I'm afraid I've had some bad news, my friends. I was doing the usual rounds in the Camorra's systems network last night, when I came across a communication between them and the Colombian gang which we annoyed so much.'

He hesitates, and Daha gently steps in. 'What Tommaso found was, in effect, his own death warrant. There is a contract out for him, and a large price on his head.'

I feel very cold. 'So, they don't believe he's in prison?'

Daha replies, 'The wording went that, wherever he is, in prison or at liberty, he is a target.'

Becks says to Tommaso, 'Do you think they guessed that you were behind Lo Coltello's arrest and the taking of the Poseidon?'

He smiles his thin smile. 'They probably don't care. They just want someone to get at because of how badly they've been damaged.'

Daha says, 'So we must act swiftly. I have the

means to protect Tommaso whilst ensuring that he sees one of the finest heart specialists in the world. He needs to disappear, and he can do that in India.'

Tommaso adds, 'I can continue to inflict damage on drugs gangs by feeding intelligence to the authorities. But our days of stealing narco-subs are over.'

I don't feel too sorry about that. 'Where will you be staying?'

Dark eyes glowing, as though he is looking at the picture his words are painting, Daha says, 'He will have his own apartment in my country house. It is very secure, discreetly guarded 24/7. My mother and father live there, and also my younger sister. And I intend to shamelessly copy Monsieur's designs and install a pumped moat …'

Tommaso finishes the sentence, 'Where there will be kingfishers, like the new Château de Montaubon. And Daha will show me how he creates his diamonds.' He looks happier than I've ever seen him before.

Daha says, 'Although I can never become a hacker of Tommaso's calibre, I will assist him in causing more upsets in the criminal community.'

Dad is looking stunned. 'When are you going?'

Monsieur replies, 'They must leave now. With delay, the risk increases.'

Daha says, 'There is a Gulfstream arriving at Marseille Marignane in one hour. The airport authorities have been most helpful in giving us an emergency slot.'

Monsieur comments, 'When I contacted the Marseille Chief of Police, he immediately understood the seriousness of the situation. They will have a police escort all the way to the plane.'

Tommaso gives Dad a huge hug. 'You needn't be worried, Uncle. I am going to be very safe in Daha's country house – and very happy.'

Hugging him back, Dad says softly, 'It's good to know that, Tommaso.'

Mum takes Dad's hand. 'And when all this vendetta rage has died down, we'll find ways of seeing each other again, won't we?'

Daha says warmly, 'Of course we will! And we will keep in touch securely through Tommaso's wiki. Now, we must be on our way.'

A few minutes later, after farewell hugs and handshakes, Becks and I watch the red Lambo kick up gravel on the drive, its V10 engine snarling. 'God I love the sound of that car!'

As the Lambo nears the slowly opening wrought iron gates, with the flashing blue lights of the police escort waiting beyond, Tommaso turns and waves. We wave back and Becks blows a kiss. 'We'll see them again.'

Instinctively, I look around for Corbo. But there's no sign of the raven. Becks takes my hand. 'If anyone can keep Tommaso safe, Daha can.'